PRAISE FOR
KRACKLE'S LAST MOVIE

"There is no other writer like Chelsea Sutton. *Krackle's Last Movie* is heart-felt, graceful, and astoundingly well-crafted. You'll be aching to reread it the moment you finish."
—Sam Asher, founder and editor of *The Cosmic Background*

"What a great story! Full of humor and wisdom and weirdness and pathos and wonder and lots of other stuff, too. Chelsea Sutton delivers the magic!"
    —Karen Joy Fowler, author of *Booth* and the New York Times
    bestseller *We Are All Completely Beside Ourselves*

"Chelsea Sutton pulls off a kind of magic trick with her novella, *Krackle's Last Movie*. Never have I read a story that so seamlessly and enjoyably wove so much mythology and monster lore together. Sutton manages to bring to her world not just monsters, but humor, pathos, humanity, and heart-wrench. Reading this novella is a pure delight."
    —Manuel Gonzales, author of *The Regional Office is Under Attack!*
    and *The Miniature Wife*

"Part mystery, part monster movie, part searing look into the shadowy cor-ners of the soul, *Krackle's Last Movie* manages to be simultaneously sensa-tional and insightful. Chelsea Sutton's novella packs more surprise twists and turns than a novel five times its length, every one of them delightful and wrapped, mummy-like, in her gorgeous language. Like all the best books, as soon as I finished it I wanted to read it again."
    —Anjali Sachdeva, author of *All the Names They Used for God*

"*Krackle's Last Movie* is a lightning bolt invitation to travel through the surreal, intimate landscapes occupied by monsters, time loss, and memory stretching. From angels with clipped wings, to mermaids, and mummies stuck in time, these characters and their relationships will weave themselves into the crevices of your heart so it will be impossible to let them go when the story ends."
—Shingai Njeri Kagunda, author of *& This is How to Stay Alive*

"A dark, clever story about the narratives we build around ourselves, that dazzles with its love for the strange and uncanny. In a novella's amount of Time and with sharp, precise prose, Chelsea Sutton weaves the language of cinema, theater, magic, religious trauma, and Time together to create a story so, so deeply sincere. Chelsea Sutton understands monsters—their pulpiness and the innate tragedy of them. *Krackle's Last Movie* is for those who have ever been made to feel ashamed of who they are."
—M. M. Olivas, author of *Sundown in San Ojuela*

KRACKLE'S LAST MOVIE

KRACKLE'S LAST MOVIE

A NOVELLA

CHELSEA SUTTON

Published by Split/Lip Press
PO Box 27656
Ralston, NE 68127
www.splitlippress.com

ISBN: 978-1-952897-48-1

Cover Art: Adrián Tre Polo
Cover and Book Design: David Wojciechowski
Editing: Kate Finegan

To everyone who has ever cried in a bathroom.

"You have been amazing. Remember that."

-The Great Merlan, The Final Performance

IT'S BEEN FIFTEEN DAYS SINCE MINERVA KRACKLE DISAPPEARED, seven days since Dr. Danger and I decided we needed to finish the cut of Krackle's latest movie before the film festival pulled our place in the line-up, and eight hours since Dr. Danger brought me a replenish of pizza and Diet Coke.

So I'm here, a slumped mess of a creature hunching over Krackle's editing bay that long ago took over her living room. Three monitors play various reels of footage, much of which I've spent the last six years capturing or digging up from archives alongside her. Interviews and found footage and an entire investigative road trip sequence documenting the passion and obsession of Krackle's life.

It's not exactly easy trying to finish someone else's life work, especially when you're wildly aware of how her first film was eaten alive by her distribution company and the press, and that she was almost murdered because of it.

Anyway, that's all part of this movie.

Krackle had been slowly editing this for ten years, since before I joined the team. And here I am, slapping together the last third as if I know what the ending is supposed to be. What Krackle wanted the ending to be.

There's a leak in the corner of the living room as I'm editing, a leak that started years ago and still going strong. It's a leak that begins where bath water drips down each time the upstairs neighbors splash over their tub, which makes the air smell like boiled fish and noodles.

Knowing the beginning of a thing doesn't mean you always know the ending. By holding a camera at Krackle's face or the face of the person we were interviewing, I thought I was making some kind of art or something, sure, but Krackle had never really been clear about where this was all going, or I had never asked and so therefore she didn't explain. I wish I had asked more questions. I wish she was here to help. I wish a lot of things.

But Krackle disappeared and didn't leave me instructions except to finish it. *It's not mine anymore anyway*, is what Krackle wrote. *Be good.*

Whatever the hell that's supposed to mean. She didn't leave a moral or a meaning or even a guideline for Time, for years to explore or ignore, for the length of the movie itself, for the length of Time I should take to read page after page of Krackle's notebooks and obsess over every word I can't quite make out, the endless sentences written vertically along the binding when she ran out of space, in deep, ink-bleeding cursive.

I know there has to be a right way to do this. Or at least I know there's a *wrong* way to do this—many wrong ways, in fact, that would make the whole project, and the lives of the people featured in it, into a joke. So that all suggests there has to be a *right* way to do this, a right way to order the interviews, to cut a moment off before an emotional breakdown, to linger on some pleading eyes or some scaled hand or bloody fang, to let a sentence hang in the air—just so—to hold the attention of an audience.

I'm going through all the road trip stuff I shot with Krackle, the whole thing with the mummy girl leading up to Krackle disappearing, plus Krackle's journals and photos, plus everything Krackle filmed over the last fifty years of her documentary work interviewing weirdos and maniacs and wannabes. And then there's the raw stuff from her first and only other movie, *The Monsters Are Here!*—you've probably heard about it, it was a colossal flop in 1997. They chopped up her footage so much that Krackle hardly recognized it.

That's not even her title. What a stupid title.

Krackle already pulled what raw footage she still had from the first film that she apparently still thought was relevant in its original form. Documentation of werewolves, invisible people, vampires, and more strange and complicated shifts in human anatomy that had sprung up in those years between 1972 and 1997. Things that went largely ignored and laughed off as either some kind of mass hysteria or mass hysteria–adjacent.

Krackle had spent those years after the first movie mostly working as a night custodian, but something made her begin conducting interviews again around 2009. Those are the interviews she had only just started to edit.

I'm in there, too. To see my six-year-younger face and have to guess what Krackle was maybe, possibly, wanting to include about me in this movie, to interlock my life with hers in this particular way, makes me wish even more that she was here, that's she'd stop being disappeared already and talk to me.

Anyway, this movie isn't about me.

Krackle wasn't a talker. She asked questions, she listened, but she seldom talked about herself. That's why so many people felt comfortable with her. Trusted her with their stories.

That's not me. I've mastered that perfect withholding fuck-off stare that keeps even the stoniest asshole at bay. I've put a lot of work into this persona, thank you.

Of course, I had to soften up a bit when on assignment with Krackle. You couldn't have your camerawoman scaring off the subjects.

My back is pounding and raw and sore, so I'm leaning close to the computer screen, my body weight on my elbows, though it doesn't matter how I sit, really, because I can always feel the skin pulling itself, peeling away, stretching to make room for something.

Anyway.

We'll get to that. That's part of the movie too.

• • • • •

(2019) VIDEO

This clip is grainy and tinted a tarnished gold and gray – like old pirate treasure, or hot embers mixing with ash, or a flashlight beam through before-dawn fog.

Minerva Krackle—age seventy-two—with long silver hair and a purple robe, is hunched over a creaky kitchen table, her cell phone sitting in front of her. She's talking to someone on speaker.

It's 5 a.m. One day before we went on the mummy hunt. Sixteen days before Krackle disappeared and I was left to finish her work.

The woman on the phone is Liz—age thirty-nine—who called Minerva back (finally) on her way to work at the local diner in her hometown of Blue Jay, California. It's raining where Liz is—you can hear the storm on the other side of her voice.

Krackle had been searching for her old camcorder while talking to Liz, finally finding it stuffed on the bookshelf between a book on the occult and a book about shape shifters.

She only turns the camcorder on after Liz admits that that modern mummy story Krackle read on those urban legend blogs is real.

So the clip starts with Krackle saying, "I'm sorry Liz, could you repeat that?"

"It's all real," says Liz. "I mean, most of it. I guess."

"Great, that's great," says Krackle. She's furiously writing things down in her journal. At this moment she's jotting down every bit of the mummy case she can remember. As I watch this bit of the video, she's flipping through the journal herself—Krackle in the past writing out her notes while I follow along with her in the future.

There's a whole box of clippings and research about the mummy in Krackle's bedroom, but she's got a bad knee and can't get back up at the moment of this video to go find it. By the time she'd get there and back, Liz would be serving truck drivers dinner instead of breakfast.

Three days after Krackle's disappearance, I would find that box of clippings. It's mostly full of rumors, strange sightings in rag papers, and a few features about the stage magician The Great Merlan, who died tragically in the middle of a show back in 2010.

The notes Krackle writes on this clip are:

Modern-day mummy of San Bernardino County.
Sister. Died young.
Won't stay dead.
Magician? Curse?

"I've tried to talk to you ever since I first heard," says Krackle.

"You should've never found out," says Liz. "But I guess that's your job."

"Sorry," says Krackle.

"Look, if you want to meet her, you have to do me a favor," says Liz.

"I don't pay for my interviews," says Krackle.

"I don't want your money," says Liz. "The truth is, Meggie doesn't want to see me, so I can't really just…introduce you."

"Meggie," repeats Krackle. Even with all the research, the phone calls, the nights traipsing through the woods looking for the mummy, this was the first time Krackle heard her name out loud.

"So you have to do something for me…for Meggie…first," says Liz. "Before you get your interview."

"Why now?" says Krackle. "I've reached out dozens of Times before."

There's a buzzing silence on the phone. The sound of rain and some sort of meat frying on a grill and the jingle of a bell on the diner door. Liz coughs. "You ever own a dog?" says Liz.

"Lots," says Krackle.

"You love them?" says Liz.

"Of course," says Krackle.

Liz sighs. "Imagine you got this dog and you don't know how you feel about it, not really, but whatever, and this dog keeps getting out of the yard. You spend weeks looking for it and you're distraught and it just consumes your whole life. Then it comes home and everything is fine again. But it keeps doing this, you see? It runs away again and again, and maybe one day it dies but you can't even feel anything because, damn it, at least you don't have to chase it anymore. And maybe you even wished it would just die already so you can get some peace. But you feel guilty about that, like maybe you willed it to die. But then the next morning, it's there in the yard again. Dead as ever but still, like, wants to play fetch."

Through this whole thing, Krackle is biting the inside of her cheek. It's something she does when she's nervous or thinking real hard. You can't tell on the clip, but that's what she's doing. She's biting so hard blood is seeping onto her tongue.

"Okay," says Krackle. The same "okay" I have heard her say in every interview. The "okay" that says, "I understand" or "I'm trying to understand, please go on. Please, please, go on."

"And so you keep playing, and you get older, and the dog doesn't age so much as start to fall apart, and even after its paws have rubbed down to stubs and its nose has cracked in half and its tongue is dried up, it still wants to play like no Time is passing at all, and you love that thing so much but also hate it and your old muscles can't take it anymore and you wonder if you're just going to keep going on like this, watching each other crumble into pieces."

"Okay," says Krackle.

"It's like that," says Liz.

●　●　●　●　●

That's how Krackle chose to start her movie, and I appreciate the clue. It tells me what we're building toward: the mummy. Krackle had heard about a mummy girl up in the mountains in Southern California, not far from Krackle's apartment in Los Angeles, and that this waitress, Liz, had something to do with it. But Liz had been avoiding her phone calls for years. Krackle had heard that the mummy had a tomb somewhere out in the woods, had even dragged me and Dr. Danger out in the middle of the night to look for it—but what does a modern tomb look like? How could you possibly know it when you see it?

I remember traipsing through the woods, only the light on my camera showing the way. I recorded every moment of that trip, not necessarily because we needed it, but because it made me feel useful. And when I don't feel useful, other bad thoughts start flooding in.

But now I'm glad I can go back and check my memory.

"Why is it so important we find this mummy?" I had asked.

Dr. Danger had a machete he was using to cut through some of the underbrush. I had tried to keep my distance from him, in case he swung a little too wide. My arms and legs were parts of my body that would not grow back.

As far as I knew.

Krackle was following behind Dr. Danger, unfazed by the blade. "What do you mean?" she said.

"I mean, why her? Why's it so important? You got plenty of footage of other people. Other interviews."

"This one's different," is all Krackle had said. "Usually interviewees come to me. But this one needs me to find her."

"How can you know that?" I said.

Krackle stopped and looked up into the trees, as if scanning the air for something. "I'm not sure," she finally said. "It's not so much that I know it's something I *need* to do…it's like I know I've already done it." And she walked forward without offering any further explanation.

Maybe two hours into that search in the woods, I thought I heard a faraway Backstreet Boys song playing deep within a particularly thick patch of trees. I stood there for a minute and let my eyes try to focus on the darkness. I thought I saw a swirling wave of light dancing to the music.

I'll admit that sometimes I see colors that don't have names yet. Colors you've never seen because, well, you can't. But because I can, I get to name them.

The color of this wave—its name is Maria.

Anyway. We didn't realize how close we were that night.

And now when I think of those woods, all I see are police hiking through the trees, searching for a confused Krackle, or a run-away Krackle, or a very, very dead Krackle.

We haven't had a check-in from the police for a couple days. Krackle had no next-of-kin, so Dr. Danger is the closest thing to family she's got. He's the emergency contact.

The leak in the corner of Krackle's apartment is getting heavier. The splashing upstairs, more regular. I take a break from the footage to change out the bucket under the leak and dump the water into the kitchen sink. In the corner of the counter is a coffee maker with stacks of pre-ground coffee packs and jars of cinnamon. I've never been a coffee drinker, but I figure maybe it's time to take it up. Krackle drank cold coffee almost constantly. So I start up the pot.

The next clip in Krackle's cut of the movie is an interview she did in 1972. It is only audio, but I know there's a journal entry for this day. I pull the oldest journals from Krackle's shelves (they are all labeled and meticulously identified, up until Krackle's last week or so). I listen to the tape and begin to scan the appropriate journal pages into the computer.

• • • • •

(1972) AUDIO

It's New York in 1972, Minerva Krackle is 25 years old with bright orange hair that frizzes in the humidity of August. This is not on the audiotape. I know this because I've now read her journals three times since she disappeared, because I'm reading them again right now as I listen to the tape, because I've gone through all her old photos, because it is my job, now, to know this.

The frizzy-haired Minerva Krackle is riding the subway, drinking coffee that has long ago grown cold, and waiting for a man to meet her, a man with one snaggletooth hanging over his lip, a bit of red liquid dripping from it. He had found her, had looked at her curiously from a coffee shop window and flagged her down. Had told her he had something he wanted to tell her, and that he would meet her on the subway.

Snaggletooth jumps on somewhere around Harlem and sits beside her. They talk, Minerva Krackle and Snaggletooth, a recorder between them, as she doesn't own a video camera of any kind at this point. The recorder creaks a little in the background of their conversation. The subway brakes squeak. People hum and occasionally shout and grumble.

She asks Snaggletooth when he realized he was a vampire.

"When candy stopped tasting like anything. When it was just air," Snaggletooth says. "Or worse. Dirt. It started tasting like dirt."

"Just candy?"

"And soda. And my mom's pot roast. And pancakes. You ever have blueberry pancakes? My mom used to make a happy face with bananas and whipped cream on top of the pancakes. On my birthday, I'd get a triple stack and triple the whipped cream."

Minerva Krackle is looking this kid up and down, noting in her journal the Mickey Mouse T-shirt with the blood stains, the mop of blonde hair covering his one glowing red eye, his other blue eye looking wet and curious. By the softness of his face, he's no older than sixteen.

"How old are you?" she asks.

"98 and a half. At least I am now. A few months ago I was sixteen. But now I'm 98 and a half."

"That's mathematically impossible," says Krackle in a friendly tone

8

that I usually only heard her use in casual conversation, never in interviews. She had shaped her interview voice over the years.

"It is strange," says Snaggletooth. "It's like I have multiple timelines in my head. One of my sixteen-year-old self. One much longer and harder to pin down. Both are me. I don't know how else to explain it."

Krackle clears her throat. I can hear Krackle's mouth curling up on the left side, her freckles somehow growing darker, her left ear twitching. Only me and Dr. Danger would know what this sounds like. I've heard it many times before and I feel special, somehow, for knowing it is there.

"Can I ask something personal?" Krackle says.

Snaggletooth giggles.

"What did it feel like to be bitten?" Krackle asks.

"Oh, I never got bitten," says Snaggletooth.

"But isn't that how you become a vampire?"

"I don't know," says Snaggletooth. His voice is getting far away here, heavy. I can almost hear the air get colder. "One day I just woke up this way. Sometimes, I guess, you don't know you're changing until suddenly, there you are."

It's here that the sound of a musical theatre student doing vocal exercises echoes through the subway and onto the tape.

Krackle had heard rumblings of a shift happening weeks before Snaggletooth flagged her down. A change. A transition of sorts. People had all sorts of words for it in the stories they'd tell of humans suddenly growing parts and pieces of monsters. Fangs or hair or fins or, sometimes, something else even more fantastical. Something that seemed to have always been there. Buried deep down.

Krackle snapped a quick photo before Snaggletooth exited toward the East Village. In the photo, Snaggletooth is mostly a blur, only his red eye in focus, looking straight into the camera.

In her journal afterward, along with the notes about his appearance, Krackle wrote that he smelled like the feeling of sucking on old pennies while standing in a janitor's closet.

● ● ● ● ●

I'm inserting a timeline into the movie, to follow the bigger path of chaos that started in 1972 and continued until today, even if most of society decided they didn't believe it ever happened and, if it did, it was over anyway. We have a tendency to do shit like that.

Anyway. Timeline.

This will place us more clearly in Time. Krackle taught me this. She believed she had a memory (Time) disorder, where pieces of her life would slip soundlessly away from her, that she would sometimes be here, sometimes in the past, sometimes in a place she didn't recognize yet—and she couldn't hold onto much of anything for very long. That's why she wrote it all down. It's why she carried a recorder with her, and later a camcorder, and on and on. There are hundreds of boxes of tapes in Krackle's home. We could make a dozen films from everything she has collected and, still, there would be parts of her life we would miss entirely.

• • • • •

(1972) TIMELINE

Five cases reported across the United States of a mysterious "beastification" that came upon people seemingly overnight. One grew a hairy back and overly pronounced canines. One seemed to be growing a horn in the middle of their forehead. One whose left half of their body became covered in hardened, scale-like skin. One whose head went invisible without warning at various times during the day (or so claimed he and his wife). One was found naked in the neighbor's pig pen, having drunk the blood of two prize heifers.

Hypertrichosis. Hormones. Bone spurs. Skin disease. Insanity. Porphyria. Explained. Noted. Filed away.

The term "curious monster" first appears in one of these original medical reports, in a note section, written in wild cursive.

• • • • •

(2013) VIDEO

The mermaids were my first assignment with Minerva Krackle. She'd agreed to take me on as an assistant and camera operator, and, to make it easy on her for my first shoot, we traveled no further than the third floor of Krackle's apartment building. Her upstairs neighbors.

Krackle chose to put this clip here, near the beginning of the movie, maybe to introduce me as a character, maybe to introduce the idea that maybe the curious monster syndrome, or CMS, which the phenomenon started to be called in the early 1980s, wasn't completely in people's imaginations or explained away as other known diseases. Maybe mermaids existed when they didn't exist before.

The clip is a bit out of focus, because the camera lens kept fogging up from the humidity in the bathroom. Minerva Krackle, age sixty-six, is laughing with two mermaids lounging in an oversized tub tinted lime green.

I knew that I was being tested. Could Krackle trust me around the people she wanted most to talk to?

It's good to remember that, even if you grow up with your own curious parts of yourself, that doesn't always make you prepared for the curiosities of others.

Everything in the bathroom is lime green—the tiles, the towels, the toothbrushes—and speckled with gold. I make sure to get a shot of the two gold-colored wheelchairs pushed against the wall. I'm shaking a little, and you can see it on the camera.

"So what's this for, anyway?" says the first mermaid, Lenore.

"Yeah, what kind of movie are you making?" says the second mermaid, Leelee, raising her eyebrow. "I hear some funny sounds coming from downstairs sometimes, Minerva."

"And I have water coming straight through my ceiling sometimes," says Krackle.

"Shit, we'll be better," says Lenore.

"No, we won't," says Leelee. "Unless your little friend gets me from my good angle."

I'm shaking partly because I can see their long and glittering tails, rainbowed and shimmering, containing more colors than the human eye can detect. There's an endlessness to those tails that I cannot capture on the camera.

I name one of those colors Harry. Another Olga. Another Anil.

"This is Harper. She's my new assistant," says Krackle. She turns to me. "What do you think?"

"Of…of…what exactly?" I say.

Lenore and Leelee cackle.

"Of our neighbors," says Krackle.

Also, they are both topless. They remind me of a tiny mermaid figurine my grandmother once brought me home from a Denmark trip she'd taken. The figurine was also topless and sat next to my Minnie Mouse alarm clock until I was thirteen.

"They have a great…sense of style," I say. I gesture around the bathroom.

Lenore and Leelee scream in delight.

"You have anything to ask them?" says Krackle.

"I'm just the camera person," I say.

"That's not a question," says Krackle.

I look at Lenore and Leelee. I have a million questions I could ask, and all seem wildly boring or wildly inappropriate. So I say, "What's your favorite food?"

Krackle smiles and keeps looking at me as the mermaids make loud thinking sounds and splash more water onto the floor and, probably, into Krackle's apartment.

"This is the thing," says Lenore, "I really love shrimp."

"And salmon," says Leelee. "I love me a good grilled salmon."

They both flick their tails and make hungry gurgles. A few drops of water land on the camera lens and I wipe them away.

"Do you suppose there's an argument that you two eating a fish is cannibalism?" says Krackle, smiling.

"Depends on if you think of us as fish," says Lenore.

"I've heard of humans who eat monkey brains," says Leelee.

"Monkeys look an awful lot like humans," says Lenore.

The mermaids are fucking with me.

You have not felt shame until you know what it feels like for mermaids to fuck with you.

"Two arms, two legs, lots of hair," says Leelee.

"Brain looks similar, too," says Lenore.

"Do you think of yourself as a monkey?" asks Leelee, looking at Krackle but winking at me.

I move closer because you can't quite see the tails in the frame, and the humidity in the room is choking both me and the camera.

"It's the point of view," says Lenore. "What high horse are you riding?"

"And do you eat the horse?" says Leelee.

More laughing, a wave of water from the tub, and the camera cuts out.

● ● ● ● ●

Dr. Danger pointed out that maybe Krackle wanted me to be a main character in this movie, which was not something she'd ever asked me about. She never got my clearance, not once. "But you were her assistant," he says.

"I *am* her assistant," I say. "We don't know she's dead."

"Okay. Whatever," he says. "But I bet you anything she wanted you to record yourself doing the…you know."

"No," I say. I'm not doing that. I refuse to.

But Dr. Danger is right. I know he's right. And I hate when he's right.

Dr. Danger pats me hard on the back. I wince. "You letting them grow?" he asks.

"Fuck off," I say, and stuff another slice of pizza in my mouth.

Dr. Danger is a supervillain. Krackle interviewed him in 1993, and he was heavily featured in her first documentary, *The Monsters Are Here!*—a fact that he does not hold against her. He has not left Krackle's side since.

I've always assumed Dr. Danger is planning to poison or freeze me or something worse, if he can think of it (but he doesn't have a particularly deep imagination). He is always offering me warm gelatin candies with taped-up wrappers, hot sodas with the labels ripped away. Keep an eye out, and you can catch him doing this on camera.

He frequently cleans his Freeze Ray gun and points it in my direction. I don't actually believe the Freeze Ray works, but I never leave him alone with food or drink I plan to consume. The pizza this week, during editing, is an exception. Because I'm desperate.

And you know what, maybe Dr. Danger poisoning me would be a great ending to the film. And he can fucking finish it himself then.

Anyway.

He's here to review what the film is so far, and we watch up until the place I have to start inserting some of the latest footage, when we went to find the mummy.

He lingers over the order of things, the choice of clips: Krackle and Liz on the phone, Snaggletooth, the mermaids, the cloud, the arms, the werewolf, the assassination.

"This is not acceptable," says Dr. Danger.

"If you have a better suggestion, let's hear it," I say.

"What does the vampire have to do with anything? What's the point of dragging up all the old interviews?" Dr. Danger opens a pizza box and starts chomping on a slice with double sausage.

"He's literally the beginning of everything," I say. "Krackle chose that clip. This isn't just about the mummy. It's about all of it."

"So you're making it about Krackle," says Dr. Danger. "It was never about her. She would be incredibly offended by this."

"It was always about her," I say. "That's how documentaries work. You can't help it."

"So, fine, then the way this is laid out is like—"

"How her mind worked," I say. "The whole Time thing she always talked about."

Dr. Danger leans back. "And it's about you."

"If it's about me, it's also about you," I say.

"Did she put my interview in this cut?" says Dr. Danger.

"Sure did," I say, taking another bite of the pizza. "She didn't get your permission either, did she?"

"Don't talk with your mouth full. You're a disgusting animal," he says.

I swallow. I want to not be offended by this. He only has a small rotation of insults and I've heard them all. I should have the skin for them by now.

To tell you the truth, I've never understood his whole supervillain thing. I don't think I could name one evil thing he's done in the years I've known him. Annoying, yes. Evil, no.

"How would you define evil?" I say. I enjoy watching Dr. Danger squirm a bit at off-topic questions. I like watching him take off his top hat and run his fingers along the brim. There is a thinning of the fabric where he rubs his fingers. He's been anxious like this since Krackle disappeared, and the hat brim is starting to come apart in that particular place he keeps touching.

"That's a stupid question," he says.

"You're a supervillain. Thought you might have an opinion," I say. "Want to know what I think it is?"

"No," says Dr. Danger, and stuffs the whole of the pizza crust in his mouth.

I sigh. The guy really is no fun at all.

"I think we're missing some pieces," I say.

"We're waiting on the video from the tomb," says Dr. Danger. "They took it for evidence but the footage might be too…I don't even know."

"The camera looked water-logged."

"It was dry," says Dr. Danger.

"I know that. I was fucking there," I say.

"Then what are we talking about?"

"We might not get the footage from the tomb…that's fine," I say.

"That's *fine?*"

"We have to do more interviews."

Dr. Danger glares at me, pizza crust soft and filling his cheeks.

"We have to find the Demon Hunter," I say.

Dr. Danger shakes his head and I hand him a list I made. The interviews we need to record ourselves, without Krackle. *Bobby Olsen. The Ghost. Liz.*

Me.

"I don't believe in ghosts," says Dr. Danger. "And Bobby's an asshole."

"I'll try to lock down Liz," I say. "You go find Bobby. And stop at the game store for a Ouija board or something."

Dr. Danger's cell phone rings. It's the police. A few mumbled exchanges later, Dr. Danger is shaking his head and I know they still haven't found her, still haven't recovered the footage. Still nothing.

We sit in silence for a long time after Dr. Danger gets off the call.

He watches me slowly edit a particularly irritating transition in the film.

Finally, he clears his throat and holds up the list I've written.

"And what about your...*interview?*" says Dr. Danger. "I can operate the camera. If you want company." He's staring at the list, not looking at me; the only sounds in the room are his chewing, the drip from the ceiling, the distant chatting of an interview still playing on one of the monitors. I know he's being kind by not looking at me.

"I'm not doing that," I say. "I'll figure out another way." Even I don't believe me.

Keeping his eyes still averted, he nods at the lumps forming on my back. "I know they hurt when you cut them off, but do they hurt when they grow back?"

"Like hell," I say.

"Good," says Dr. Danger.

● ● ● ● ●

(1963) AUDIO

Minerva Krackle visits a psychic at age sixteen and hides a recorder in her handbag. This is less to do with investigative journalism and more to do with Krackle not wanting to forget what she's told. Though extensive testing has turned up nothing, young Minerva suspects she has an undiagnosed memory disorder. She believes she has forgotten most of her life already and does not want this to continue. It is mostly a feeling of dark voids, of clouds in her thoughts, things that blur and overlap the moments in a day. She wants to know each second, not just the accumulation of seconds. If she misses the details then, she suspects, she will miss the big picture.

She has taken up journaling and recording much of her life as a backup plan to her own mind. She spends an hour each night going over the details of the day. Reviewing the tapes when her memory falters. At this moment, there are three shoeboxes worth of tapes in her closet.

She pays particular attention to the smells. Smells are where true memory lives, Minerva says in her journals. Smell is often the first impression and the last bit to disappear.

Krackle writes in her journal, afterward, that the psychic's room smelled of boiled spinach and hemp, and there was a small cloud that hovered right below the ceiling. The cloud had no particular scent that Minerva Krackle had been acquainted with, but it seemed to produce a low hum that she did not catch on her recording.

"You'll have a very…splashy career," says the psychic.

Minerva Krackle, who at this moment believes she will become a neurosurgeon specializing in the anatomy of memory, clears her throat. Splashy doesn't seem like a great word for a doctor. "Doing what?" she asks.

"Movies," says the psychic.

"Let me guess, you think I want to be an actress? Go off to Hollywood and marry Rock Hudson and all that?"

"You're a terrible actress," says the psychic. "You're too strange for that. That's probably why they'll talk to you."

Krackle doesn't ask the psychic who "they" are.

I can hear Krackle swallow and bite her cheek as I listen to the tape again, for the tenth time, far in the future, wondering if this is a good moment to introduce this cloud of hers. Is this a good point in the movie? Too early? Already too late?

"Your last movie's climactic scene will be underwater," says the psychic. "Hope you know how to swim because otherwise…you know."

"I don't know," says Krackle. "That's why I'm here."

"I'm insinuating you might die," says the psychic with a long sigh.

"Insinuating or telling me?" says Krackle.

"It's what I *see*," says the psychic.

"I've never learned to swim and don't plan to," says Krackle, glancing quickly up at the ceiling, trying to see the cloud without the psychic noticing. I know this from the click in Krackle's neck which was always there when she craned her neck back. I can hear that same click in future interviews—the half bug/half man who climbed to the ceiling during their interview, the giant who loved top hats, the woman who claimed that her stench was strong enough to kill men within six seconds and insisted Krackle interview her while the woman stayed on her balcony, and Krackle stood in her driveway, peering up into the sun.

"You brought that thing in here with you," says the psychic. "Don't blame that on me."

"What are you talking about?" says Krackle.

"The cloud, genius," says the psychic. "You really are a terrible actress."

"What is it?" says Krackle. She whispers this, as if to keep the cloud from hearing. Her voice is suddenly serious, slightly panicked. I can hear the psychic snort a laugh and lean back in her creaking chair.

"That'll be five bucks extra," says the psychic, "or figure it out yourself."

"Screw you," says young Minerva Krackle. "I don't believe in psychics anyway."

"As if believing has anything to do with it," says the psychic.

And Krackle is gone.

She would later write in her journal that she didn't have another five dollars, that she'd spent everything she had on the basic reading and the jug of milk that she'd promised her mother she'd pick up on her way home.

Krackle would always keep an extra five dollars in her pocket from then on, even when sleeping. But that bit of detail is not in the movie.

● ● ● ● ●

I hadn't expected that so many scenes in this movie would take place in the bathroom.

I've hunched in this bathtub so many times in the years since I started working for Krackle. There is a slight, barely noticeable tint of red soaked into the fiberglass. In the early years, I'd do this at my own apartment, in private, but then we had enough late nights or long out-of-town weeks that I'd forget to keep up with the maintenance and Krackle would insist I just take care of it here, where she could help dress the wounds properly.

I only let Krackle watch me once. I don't like the idea of putting this part of my life in the movie.

I tell myself I can delete it from the final cut whenever I want. Before I send it off.

I can delete it.

I will.

Probably.

I tape over my breasts and set the camera up on a stool. I mark out on the tub where I need to be to stay in frame, then sit with my back toward the camera.

I have let them grow bigger than usual. Dr. Danger was right. The lumps are protruding easily six inches from my shoulder blades right now, the wings slicing out already another twelve. There are always feathers at this length, and the colors remind me of the mermaids' tails upstairs—black, but full of colors, more colors than you can see. I named a few of these colors when I was a kid just getting into dolls. Barbie and Ken and Stacy. But there are new ones today.

Krackle once asked if I would grow them to full size one day and show her how I flew with them. But I had not grown them to their full length since I was four years old. I had no idea how big they could get or needed to get to hold me. The muscles have been cut and regrown so often, I'm not sure they would even work anymore. I've never used them. They don't even feel like they belong to me.

And I don't understand why their removal needs to be so messy. I try not to think of the pieces of me falling into the tub as I chop myself away.

In the video, you see me cutting into my lumps methodically. You see feathers unlatch and spiral out of frame. You see blood spill down my back slowly, like it's done this before, countless times, because it has. You see me pulling at the last strands of muscle and bone fibers I can barely reach, until there are just two stumps of flesh, low enough to be easily hidden under loose clothing. Throughout the segment, you can hear me screeching, not exactly like a bird, something just beyond it, a flying creature drowning in the air.

I don't remember making those sounds. I always thought of myself as fantastically stoic.

Once it is all removed, I sit for a long time, back to the camera, forehead leaning on the cool of the tile wall, letting the blood dribble down into the bathtub.

You can't see this, but I start to cry at this point, but not because of the pain. The pain I'm used to. But I realize Krackle isn't here to help me out of the tub. Krackle isn't here to help me clean up the mess I've made. I realize that I've come to depend on that part of the ritual. And I hate her for it.

At the end of this clip, the part that ends up in the movie, anyway, I look up toward the ceiling, near the right corner of the room. Some in the audience of this movie might think I am contemplating what I have done to myself, perhaps looking for help from the universe or a god, eyes searching the air where I've never been able to fly. Or, some say, maybe looking for the cloud that followed Krackle around.

But really, I just noticed that there's a leak in this part of the ceiling too. I'll have to tell the neighbors.

It's Dr. Danger who dresses my wounds this time.

• • • • •

(2019) VIDEO

It's that time in the film for the road trip content.

It's the morning after Krackle's phone call with Liz. Krackle, Dr. Danger, and I are driving down the 15 freeway to an inland suburb called Murrieta. Dr. Danger is the squat man in a top hat driving the car. Krackle is in the passenger seat. I'm in the back— the cameraperson in the jean jacket with holes in the elbows, who you only see when I turn the camera on myself for a well-timed eye-roll or frown.

Krackle is pointing to a map and speaking into the camera.

"Liz told me that a piece of the mummy is buried in one of these parks around a drainage ditch. If we want to meet the mummy, then we have to gather the pieces for her."

"How did the mummy get cut to pieces?" says Dr. Danger. "Axe? Cleaver? Scissors?"

"Liz didn't mention the how," says Krackle.

"Liz did this herself?" I say from behind the camera. "Then why isn't she the one hunting for body parts?"

"She's tried before," says Krackle. "But she can't find them. She says it's like they are hiding, like they don't want to be found…by her, at least."

Krackle points to a little patch of land circled in red. "This is the location where she thinks she buried a box but couldn't recover it herself."

"The park is huge. How will we know where to look?" I ask.

"There's a sound we have to follow," says Krackle.

"How helpful," I say, rolling my eyes into the camera quickly and then focusing back on Krackle.

"Escaping," says Krackle. "That's what Liz says it sounds like. Like escaping."

The park is below street level, hidden by groupings of trees in the middle of a housing tract. A dirt path connects to the sidewalk and quickly dips down an incline.

The rows of houses surrounding the park are an odd mix of Mediterranean and New England architecture and completely silent. It is the middle of a Tuesday, so there are no kids, no lawnmowers, no cars. Only the distant sound of a sprinkler pointing the wrong direction and watering a sidewalk, the brown lawn behind it watching in anguish.

I catch the eye of a woman in a second-floor bedroom window. She is dressed in a white nightgown, dark hair flowing to her waist. I turn the camera toward her but she ducks out of the way. All you see on the video is an empty window. The camera shakes a little here because I get a sudden chill I can't control.

We climb down to the bottom of the park, and Krackle makes everyone stand completely still and listen. The only sounds are the hum of the camera, some birds in the eucalyptus trees, and the haggard breathing of Dr. Danger, who has a pretty prominent beer gut that he sucks in with an old Victorian corset.

And then we hear it. Well, Krackle hears it first. She always picked up on these things minutes, hours, sometimes days before me or Dr. Danger.

Krackle leads Dr. Danger and me to the base of a sickly eucalyptus, the usual fragrance of the tree sappy and rotting in our noses. We can hear a scratching sound, rhythmic and aching, fingernails on metal. Krackle asks Dr. Danger to dig toward the sound. A shovel had not been anticipated nor brought, but Dr. Danger obliges nonetheless, kneeling in his corset and well-pressed slacks, and digs his hands into the sandy dirt.

I hold Dr. Danger's top hat for him.

After about four feet of digging, Dr. Danger unearths an aluminum box with two mummy arms tied together and stuffed inside. The mummy arms are wrapped in modern bandages and plastic wrap, and they cower together at the sudden opening of the lid. The right arm has a tattoo of what looks to be a white rabbit, now moldy and peeling. A few knotted friendship bracelets hang on the left arm's wrist. Both hands had been scraping at the box with their non-bandaged fingertips, the fingernails long worn down, the fingers now stubs, the tops of bone sticking out through the tips. Bone fragments cover the bottom of the box.

Here, the camera wiggles a bit because I am choking down vomit, something that comes as a big surprise to me, if I'm going to be honest. Bigger than finding mummy arms in a suburban park.

Close-up of the arms.

Shaking of the camera.

I throw up, and the camera falls at an angle that just captures Minerva Krackle's face, which is not wincing or worried or even in the usual scrunched up grimace when she bites her cheek. She takes a sip of her long-cold coffee in her travel mug.

Krackle is smiling. Her eyes wide and watery. Her hair is billowing like Wonder Woman on the top of a skyscraper.

When I recover, I yank the camera up to shoot what is happening across the park. Dr. Danger is tackling the arms, still tied together, which have sprinted on their finger bones toward the street.

"Time to get the others," says Krackle. She shoves the top of the box into the camera's view and points to a set of coordinates taped inside.

"There are more arms?" I ask, my voice full of last night's chili dinner.

"No," says Minerva. "Feet."

• • • • •

The leak is getting worse. So I go upstairs and bang on the mermaids' front door.

"Leelee! Lenore!" I say.

"Harper!" they scream back in unison.

I can smell the salt water, the fishy stench straight through the door. "There's a leak in my ceiling," I say.

"I'm no good with ceilings," says Leelee through the door.

"Yes, we're really more floor girls," says Lenore.

"You know, like the sea floor," says Leelee.

"Have you ever noticed the sea has a floor but no ceiling?" says Lenore.

"The original open concept," says Leelee.

"I don't think that's what that means," says Lenore.

"Just stop splashing so much," I say. "I don't want anything damaging Krackle's work. That's…that's all." Silence beyond the door. "Thanks."

I turn to go, but the door swings open. Leelee and Lenore are there, in their gold wheelchairs, their long fins curved and slowly flapping, their scales shining with green and gold glints today in the fluorescent light of the hall, but I keep myself from looking for any new colors I can name. Their hair appears perpetually dry and perfectly curled despite almost always being in water, despite the thick humidity of the air. This is the quietest I've ever seen them, which disturbs me. The worst thing I could ever imagine. Their silence.

"Honey, have you heard anything yet?" says Leelee.

"Any word from Minerva?" says Lenore.

"She's a missing person," I say. "Pretty sure the police will hear before me. And they haven't heard anything. There's no trace. Like she just dissolved."

"She's just gone on a lark," says Leelee. "She does that now and again."

"At least she did when she was younger," says Lenore.

"Come inside," says Leelee.

The apartment is sticky with seaweed and fish bones. I sit on a plastic-covered armchair that still seems to be damp despite the slip. Lenore serves me a cup of warm salt water while Leelee stretches herself out on the couch.

"How are you holding up, dear?" says Lenore.

I sniff the sea water but don't drink. "I'm trying to get this movie together. I can't miss the film festival deadline. Krackle worked for months to get accepted. Calling old contacts, talking people up. It has to be finished. This was her comeback."

"Yes, she's been very dedicated," says Lenore.

"For years," says Leelee. "I never thought she was going to try to finish it. Again."

"Maybe just leave it for when she gets back," says Lenore.

"Unless we're the stars. Are we the stars?" says Leelee.

I smile. Yes, I tell them. They are the stars. They giggle and my mind wanders to the tape from the tomb, the one the police are trying to recover for evidence, the footage that could tell me exactly what happened if we could just get it to play.

"Oh! Did you meet that handsome seaman?" says Lenore. "The one we told you about?"

"The one who runs the hardware store," says Leelee.

"Living in the desert. What a wild man. What a rebel," says Lenore.

"A real *catch*, that one," says Leelee. And they laugh and laugh.

I swallow a mouthful of warm sea water and let my eyes fill with tears and my mouth go dry.

● ● ● ● ●

(1964) WRITTEN RECORD: KRACKLE'S DIARY

I'm not special in any way. I have an average shoe size. And average weight. My grades are average. If there is a measurement of any kind, I'm right on the average. If there's a bell curve, I'm right in the middle. I have a worse than average memory, and that is my only claim to originality, and the only reason I write so much in you as I do. I aim to take more photos, to record more conversations. Because there are people in this world that are surprisingly unaverage, but they go unnoticed. In fact, they hope for as much. But I see them plain as day. A cloudy day.

Sometimes my memory slips feel more like Time travel, if there were such a thing. I get these glimpses of things, like clouds part and suddenly the sun is there and then suddenly it is gone again.

Do you think there are special parts of each of us that we all work our whole lives to keep secret? I don't mean just the embarrassing, bad, or let's say even evil parts of ourselves. I mean we keep the good stuff down too. The moments of genius that make us decidedly unaverage, even briefly. It's like we hold our breaths until our lives are over, hoping we won't draw attention, that no one will notice us until we choke on our own Time.

· · · · ·

(1990) TIMELINE

Mass hysteria is blamed for the deformities, the shift in personalities, the unexplained phenomenon that people experience (or cause) after quick evolution or growth or degeneration, depending on how you look at it.

Those claiming anything particularly strange are turned away after reports of thousands of prankers have been showing up at emergency rooms and urgent cares with painted patterns on their skin, Halloween masks and prosthetics, illusions that set off the sprinklers or shut down power, or otherwise cause chaos among the sick. People go to jail. People are shot in the streets. People in need of emergency care die, waiting for attention.

Anyone deemed CMS, whether an official or self-diagnosis, goes underground.

· · · · ·

(2019) VIDEO

Krackle, Dr. Danger, and I are driving into the desert, the windows rolled down, hot wind whipping through the car. Dr. Danger has his top hat pushed as far down on his head as possible without covering his eyes. I pan the camera along the landscape. Minerva Krackle has her arm out the window, her hand open, palm rounded, catching balls of air. Hold and release.

We stop at a hardware store to buy a shovel. I don't bring the camera inside. The shelves of the store are covered in dust, the greasy years sitting in the walls, and when I emerge from the back, shovel in hand, Krackle is standing at the cash register talking to the clerk, whose right arm is a long green tentacle curling around the countertop, its suckers sticking and unsticking themselves from the cracking wood.

I leave the shovel at the counter and run to get the camera.

The clip is dark, but I'm hurriedly pointing a work light toward the clerk's face.

"How long ago did we talk?" asks Krackle.

"'94 or so."

"That's right. That's right," says Krackle.

"Who's this?" I ask, short of breath and behind the camera.

"Bennie the sea monster," says the clerk. He laughs.

"A sea monster in the desert," says Krackle, laughing too.

"It's not as strange as you'd think," says Bennie the sea monster and hardware store clerk. "There's lots of weirdoes out here."

"Lenore and Leelee mentioned you," I say, forgetting for a second that I'm the cameraperson, not meant to speak. And there's a long silence that follows this statement in which I think: *fuck. I fucked it all up.*

Bennie's face breaks into a smile. "I haven't heard from those ladies in quite some time. How do you know them?"

I look at Krackle, but she's not looking at me, and I take that as a sign to shut the hell up.

"They're neighbors," says Krackle to Bennie, not me. "Got quite a crush on you."

"You shouldn't have shown them my interview," says Bennie. "I was much more handsome then. I couldn't possibly meet them now looking like this." He runs his human hand through his hair and smiles for the camera.

"I thought my interview with you might have been my last. Remember that underwater room we met in?"

"Oh boy, we were just asking for trouble."

In the present moment in the desert, I hadn't heard the audio from Minerva's psychic visit yet, so I did not see the significance of death underwater.

"When I miss the ocean, I just let myself sit on the porch and cry," says Bennie. "A good cry always does the trick. Natural salt water, you know. Makes me feel less lonely. I really hate being alone with all my thoughts. Someone my age should never be alone with his thoughts."

"You can't be older than…what?" Krackle was careful to never guess ages.

"I'm fifty-five this month," says Bennie, chin up.

"No. You don't look older than thirty-five, Bennie. Come off it," says Krackle.

Bennie leans on the counter so he has to peer up at Krackle, for a little extra drama. "That's because I'm actually older than Time itself, Minerva. I crawled out of the sea ten millennia ago and I intended to live until the ocean finds me again, out here in the dust."

A silence settles over the room and Krackle waits to see where this is going. Bennie keeps staring, a small smile forming at the corner of this mouth. He glances at my camera and winks. He doesn't seem to be affected by my fuck-off stare.

"So how many zeros would that be?" says Krackle. "I want to make sure I write your proper age in my journal."

A beat before Bennie starts laughing. "Give a guy a break and only put, let's say, six zeros, okay?"

About now I'm feeling my cheeks flush. A second tentacle of Bennie's is curling along the floor toward my feet, and he looks into the camera again—no wink, just a long stare—his eyes making me want to know all of it—all the bad things he ever did, and all the good—but I keep silent. I try to disappear behind the camera.

Bennie joins us for the next leg of the trip—to find the mummy feet—as he's never met a mummy before, or even a small piece of one.

The whole ride, the mummy arms continue to scrape inside their box. There is a wet stench coming from the box that has gotten stronger since we picked them up; I expected mummified arms to be dry, but these were soaked with something. I keep shooting from the backseat, trying to ignore Bennie's three tentacles (I count them as soon as he moves away from the counter) feeling all the corners of the car and brushing against my legs, my arms and, once, one of the growing lumps on my back.

In an unremarkable piece of desert off a dirt road, Krackle points to a looming cactus, shaped as perfectly as a cartoon drawing of itself. Again we listen for the sound. This time, it is a banging against metal. *Bang. Clang. Bang.*

Dr. Danger digs with the shovel and Bennie digs with his tentacle arms, which seem to be strong enough that just one of them could break my neck quickly and painfully. A cloud of sand puffs up around them, and I try to shield the camera lens.

Minerva Krackle is writing in her journal the whole time. Notes about Bennie, about shovels, about the heat and the smell of the desert, like human skin drying in a dusty barn.

Dr. Danger and Bennie pull another metal box to the surface. *Bang. Clang. Bang.*

Inside the box is a pair of mummy feet, taking turns kicking the inside of the box. The little toe on the left foot has a toe ring with an emerald. The big toes on both feet are worn down to nubs from years of kicking a metal box.

I swallow this time and do not vomit.

Bennie holds up the feet with his human hand and tickles them with a tentacle. The feet wiggle and a couple more toes break off, bounce off Bennie's tennis shoes, and disappear under a prickly bush.

Dr. Danger turns the car radio up full blast, an upbeat country tune that rattles the car's speakers. Bennie holds the feet up and they dance in the air, the bandages around the ankles loosening with each vibration.

On the drive back, Krackle is examining the feet in the backseat with Dr. Danger on camera duty. I'm driving us back to the hardware store and Bennie is beside me. I can feel him staring.

"So what's your deal?" says Bennie.

You can't see this on camera, but you can hear it, the question somewhere buried beneath Krackle's explanation of the feet, her list of observations of slow decay and continued animation. I say, "What do you mean?"

"I can tell when I'm talking to someone who's…well…like me," he says.

"I'm not a monster. Sorry. Sea monster," I say.

Bennie laughs. "What do they call us these days? Still curious or something else?"

"No one calls me anything," I say.

"Well, that's too bad," he says. One of his tentacles glides up my side to my back and curls around my right stump. The sensation startles me and I nearly run off the road.

"Get control of yourself, girl!" says Dr. Danger. "We have to restart a whole section now. Use your brain."

"Sorry," I say.

"I never let anyone touch these when they first appeared," says Bennie, holding up his tentacles. "It hurt, for someone to touch them, you know?"

The desert road is long and hypnotizing in front of me. The ghost of his tentacle curling again and again on my back keeps stinging me, even though he has retreated to his side of the car.

"I'm just saying, maybe that's not how it should be all the time. Forever," he says.

"You keeping your arms to yourself works fine for me," I say. But my voice breaks.

It's another forty minutes back to the hardware store, and Dr. Danger and Krackle are working the whole time while Bennie's tentacle slowly, very slowly, returns to my back, twirling and twirling under my shirt.

I don't stop him.

This is not in the movie.

We leave Bennie back at the hardware store, but not before he pours Krackle a fresh cup of coffee from the back office and drops a few ice cubes in it. Krackle sits in the front seat, watching the ice cubes melt, as I get a great angle out the back window of the car, Bennie waving his tentacle arms after us.

● ● ● ● ●

(2019) VIDEO

This clip is warm and dreamy, shot in the almost dusk light filtering through the broken blinds of Krackle's apartment. Despite the mermaids' conservative splashing, the apartment is still foggy from humidity.

I'm hunched over the creaky kitchen table, my cell phone sitting in front of me. I'm talking to someone on speaker. It's been two days since Dr. Danger and I decided to do more interviews. I've been waiting for Liz's call. Dr. Danger is off tracking down Bobby Olsen and a Ouija board. The wings on my back have already started to grow back and you can see them poking through Krackle's purple robe, which I wrapped around myself after a sudden chill ran through my body. The wings always make me cold in the first few days of growth. They are raw and a little bloody as they rip through the barely new skin. They feel like they are growing back faster. There's a heap of gauze between them and the robe to keep me from ruining it. In case Krackle comes back. When she comes back.

The woman on the phone is Liz, calling from the diner during her pre-dinner slump.

I had not anticipated Liz's call and fumbled with my camera for a minute before settling down.

The clip starts with me saying, "I'm sorry Liz, could you repeat that?"

"I don't think there's anything more to talk about," says Liz.

"Krackle saved your sister," I say. "I think you owe us just a few more minutes."

"Technically, Minerva killed Meggie," says Liz.

"Isn't that what you wanted?" I say.

Liz is silent.

"That's why you cut off her feet and arms, isn't it? You wanted her dead." I had imagined Liz ripping off Meggie's limbs many times over. There was a satisfying anger that boiled up in me imagining the act more brutal and bloody than it ever could have been in real life. "You tore your sister apart so that you could finally be rid of her."

When Liz speaks, her voice sounds smaller. Almost as if she were across the room from the telephone. "I don't owe you an explanation," she says.

"You got what you wanted, didn't you?" I say.

"Not exactly," says Liz.

"Or is it what the stage magician The Great Merlan wanted?" I say. "Did she mess up Meggie's spell so badly that she wanted her wiped away?"

The sound of dishes and voices filter through on Liz's end. "She's dead," says Liz. "Can't we just leave it alone? I don't want to talk about her anymore."

"Which one? Meggie or your old boss?" I say.

Liz snorts. "Both. I guess."

"Look. Meggie wasn't a monster. She was a scared young girl who didn't know what was happening to her. And I just want her represented…correctly. In the final film. We need to talk."

"I know my sister wasn't a monster," says Liz.

"So we're in agreement," I say. "This is the last time. Last interview."

"She wasn't a monster, but a monster created her," says Liz.

"Now we're getting somewhere," I say.

"And you're the one interviewing me?" says Liz.

"Krackle is still missing," I say.

A sigh from the phone. More dishes and wind. A jingle of the bells above the diner doors.

"Tomorrow," says Liz. "Ten o'clock. P.M." And she hangs up.

• • • • •

(1982) VIDEO: FOUND FOOTAGE

The first official footage of The Great Merlan appears on a local Vegas TV station, KTNV, just days before he is set to open what is going to be a long-running and popular stage magic show at the Sands Hotel and Casino.

Already, a group of fans are waiting around the block to buy tickets. Fans who have been following The Great Merlan since he started performing back in the 1970s. Fans who like to call themselves *Maggies* (magician groupies). The Great Merlan is in his full get-up, a tuxedo with a colorful pocket square and subtle glitter on his cheeks. He's only forty-two years old here, streaks of stylish gray across his dark hair, his bright blue eyes giving him an otherworldly look. He is still fit beneath his jacket and waistcoat, which are pulled tight against his muscles.

"So how do you do these tricks of yours?" asks the journalist with a wry smile. "Tell us some of your secrets."

"Oh, you know very well that a magician can never reveal the source of his magic!" says The Great Merlan with a grin.

"Well, give us a little tease," says the journalist, clearly flirting despite himself.

"All right, I'll say this," says The Great Merlan, and he looks into the camera, as if looking into the eyes of every single person at home.

"Time is shapeless. Time cannot be traveled or created. It can simply be rearranged," he says. "Time does not stop. It is not traveled. It is moved. And when it is moved in just the right way, it reveals what was once hidden. What was once impossible. It reveals what is waiting. Inside you. Right now."

A thousand viewers swoon.

The Great Merlan's stage show was sold out for 113 weeks in a row.

• • • • •

(2014) VIDEO

This is the one interview Krackle did with me. It was early enough in my employment with her that I felt I couldn't say no.

We shot the interview on the back patio of the apartment building, a communal space that can be reserved for private gatherings, an hour or two at a time. Krackle's reasoning was that the movie needed some different landscapes besides dingy, dark rooms. Krackle wanted someone to talk out in the sunlight.

So this moment is bright and colorful, the stucco wall behind me a warm beige with an assortment of ceramics from Mexico hanging next to NO GLASS ALLOWED and CLEAN UP AFTER YOURSELF signs. It is the opposite, I realize, of my bathroom video.

"When was the first time you cut them off?" says Krackle.

I'm visibly uncomfortable on camera, having already answered at least five previous questions about my wings before this one. To have wings at all felt like one kind of vulnerability. To have people know I ripped them away every two weeks or so, that was another.

"I think I was four," I say. "I didn't cut them off. That was my parents."

"What do you remember from that time?" says Krackle.

"I remember thinking it was bathtime," I say. "And then my dad brought in these pruning shears. The ones he used in the yard. He liked to make our shrubs look like different things. Like cats. Or horses."

"But this wasn't bathtime," says Krackle.

"They'd asked some doctor friends of theirs. They didn't want to bring me into a real doctor, in case I was taken away or...whatever." I say. "But the doctors told them how to remove the wings at home safely, how to make sure I didn't get an infection."

"How'd they do that?" says Krackle.

"Well, they cut a little too much off the first time," I say. "So they had to cauterize the wound. But otherwise, I think, just the normal stuff. Iodine. You know."

"That sounds painful."

"I don't know," I say. "I passed out after the second one was cut off so I don't know what they did after that. Just what they told me." I look away from the camera.

"Did they know the wings would grow back?" says Krackle.

"No one knew anything," I say. "So they just treated them like some kinda birth defect. Something to trim off and forget about."

"But it wasn't that easy," says Krackle.

"We kept doing it like that, like the doctors said, for at least a year or two. But my parents got fed up because everything the doctors said to do didn't work. So they let the wings grow out as big as they could while still being able to cover them easily enough. And then they brought me to their pastor," I say. "And he helped them cut them off again. Did a new baptism. Said I was some kind of earthly angel and this would help all the pain I must feel from being removed from heaven. But that I must be holy." I smile because I remember that I got a lot of candy that week, when I was holy. I watched movies and stayed home from school and life was good.

I don't say any of this.

"And what happened when they continued to grow back, over and over?" says Krackle.

I look into the camera. "Well I was obviously evil," I say. "And everything that comes with that."

"Like what?"

"Like making sure that cutting off the wings was extra painful. I think the reasoning was…if the body was in enough pain, it would reject the foreign objects growing on me. It would fight them off."

"Solid logic," Krackle says. She's trying to make me smile.

But I'm thinking about the number of times I stood in front of the congregation on a Sunday morning, the pastor splashing holy water on me, people falling in the aisles in tears, praying for me.

"Do you know what they did with the pieces they cut off you?" says Krackle.

I shrug. I don't know, actually. Part of me wonders if they buried the pieces in a mass grave that they added to every week out in our backyard. Or if they fed the pieces to our dog. Or if they just threw them away with the rest of the kitchen garbage. I never asked. I wonder if the church ever did human sacrifice rituals.

I once found the dog gnawing on a bone that looked bigger than any chicken wing was ever expected to be.

There's a silence, and you can hear an echo of voices from within the building behind me, a group of neighbors who will, in just a few minutes, come screeching drunkenly out the back door, rushing clumsily to the barbeque, a plate of raw steaks held above their heads in celebration.

"What else were they supposed to do?" I say.

• • • • •

What I don't say in that interview is how I dispose of myself once I take that job over from my parents.

There is never any ritual, no holiness to it. If I cut the flesh up into small enough chunks, or if it is soft and new enough, I flush each bit down the toilet one by one. Other times I threw it in the trash, mixing it with chicken bones and skin from dinners. For about a year, I got really into composting. You see the pattern.

• • • • •

(1991) VIDEO
The tiki bar is dark and loud and the walls are covered in fake palm tree branches. The camera Minerva Krackle sets up blasts a single harsh light onto the face of a man with a straggly beard, a hooped nose ring, and yellow eyes. He runs his hands through puffy brown and gray-speckled hair, and his shadow bounces around the wood-paneling and the stuffed parrot behind him. His T-shirt, a vintage Star Trek design, has been stitched up in several places along the arms and neck, as if it has been ripped apart multiple times.

Minerva Krackle sits just outside the light, her figure a dark smudge on the right side of the screen. There's a misty kind of cloud hovering above both of them, which, at first viewing, I thought was just cigarette smoke. But Krackle notes down in her journal later that there were no smoking-related smells in the bar. Only dried-up beer and sweat.

After pleasantries and an ordering of drinks, Krackle asks, "So when's it supposed to happen?"

"'Bout an hour," says the straggly man. "I've never had anyone watch before." There is a row of shot glasses on the table next to him. He takes one.

"I'm sure it's beautiful, John," says Krackle.

"There's nothing beautiful about it," says John the scraggly man. "I twist up into an animal. I split in two."

"What's that like?" asks Krackle.

"I had a kid once," says John the scraggly man. "Little girl."

"What was her name?"

"That's not important." John's eyes are squinting against the light. He shifts in his seat so the heat of the lamp only hits his right cheek. "She died. So. The name's not....Never mind."

"I'm sorry to hear that." Minerva takes another drink and waits.

"No. No no no. No." John the scraggly man shakes his head. A bit of dust lifts up from his beard. "I know what you're thinking. But it's not my fault."

"I know, John," says Krackle. She places her hand on John's arm and pats him softly. "Go on."

John takes another shot. Then one more. "Imagine your arm being ripped off, or a leg, or a knee. Yeah, a knee, something that connected you with something else, that made you function. It's just ripped off for no reason. You sit on one side of the room and a piece of you sits on the other, and you can't communicate anymore. No matter what you do, the fingers on that severed hand aren't going to wiggle."

"Okay," says Krackle. She takes another drink. Glances up at the cloud above them.

"So when I change it's like I'm watching my arm strangle people and punch through walls and cause all this damage and I can't do anything about it. And I know that's not me. And sometimes it maybe paints a pretty picture or mixes a drink and is real nice, but I know that's not me either. All I can do is watch."

"So that's being a werewolf?" asks Krackle.

"That's being anything," says John the scraggly man. "That's being anything."

About an hour later Minerva Krackle records John the scraggly man as he changes. He's locked in a cage in the woods across from the bar. The full moon is bigger than Krackle's ever recorded it. John as a werewolf is not much changed from John himself at first glance. Hairier, longer and sharper teeth, a long string of drool dribbling continuously from his mouth. But his face is still John's, and he whimpers in the corner most of the night as Krackle feeds him pieces of salami and cheese.

This is the interview I've watched the most. The way his body contorts into the change. I can feel my body doing the same thing. And there's this one color in his fur—I call it Irene—that is the most beautiful thing I've ever seen.

I've watched this clip thirty-two times since Krackle's disappearance. At least ten more before I finish the movie. At least.

At least.

• • • • •

(1990) WRITTEN RECORD: KRACKLE'S DIARY

When I'm conducting these interviews, I am never in one place. I shift from their childhood until their death, dropping into the days before their change, then into the moment they knew, for sure, that their body, their mind, and their life would never be the same.

It's a matter of seconds when I see this moment. I know when to be quiet and what to ask when their silence goes on for too long. But as soon as the camera is off and I'm walking away, I forget all of it. Perhaps because one person is not supposed to hold onto whole libraries of lives in one brain. But some of those moments in Time are warm, comforting. Some of it wraps itself so snuggly around you that walking away from it tears some piece of you away. So that you leave yourself in the past, entering the future lighter, but less whole.

· · · · ·

Krackle always capitalized Time.

· · · · ·

(1992) TIMELINE

The Great Merlan, now age fifty-two, goes on television to announce that he is closing his very popular Vegas show and also canceling his national tour.

"It's time The Great Merlan name was passed on to someone new. A bright new talent, someone who has followed me for some years and has trained with me and some trusted advisors. I can't wait for you to meet her," he says, smiling into the news cameras.

"But you are The Great Merlan," says the journalist. "How could we ever accept another one?"

"In a matter of months, you won't even remember my face," says The Great Merlan. "You will not know another Great Merlan before the one you will meet very soon. I promise." He winks into the camera. The gray streaks in his hair have expanded, wrinkles have formed around his eyes, but otherwise he looks younger than the day he opened his stage show. Timeless, one might say.

"You won't even realize you miss me," he says to us. "I'll take care of all of it."

Two curious monsters were found hiding in an abandoned warehouse in Fort Lauderdale. Another five in a basement in Des Moines. A few kids being homeschooled in Sacramento. They disappear.

· · · · ·

(1997) VIDEO: FOUND FOOTAGE

Four months after the release of Minerva Krackle's first movie, *The Monsters Are Here!*, she is walking out of a shopping mall in Southern California, a new camera and tapes in a bag, Dr. Danger by her side. Her red hair is graying at the roots, silver and red mixing together, catching the sunlight.

The footage is taken from a camera crew of a local news station, who have clamored up to stick a microphone in Krackle's face.

Why did you publicly condemn your distribution company?

Did you really think you were doing a documentary?

Do you really think monsters exist?

Then gunshots.

The people in the mall parking lot, screaming, ducking.

Blood splatter on asphalt.

Dr. Danger taking out his Freeze Ray and searching the parking lot for the shooter. A white van skidding away and Dr. Danger running after it, though his short legs can't take him very far.

Minerva Krackle rushed to the hospital.

Cut to news footage about a man named Bobby Olsen, a self-proclaimed demon fighter, a soldier for good. Descriptions of the damage he did to Minerva Krackle's body: one bullet straight through the knee, one bullet straight through the shoulder, one bullet straight through her left lung, inches from her heart.

Footage of Dr. Danger sitting outside Minerva's hospital room for days. For weeks.

I'm six years old when I see this on television. I have already been cut to pieces in the bathroom 111 times. I will lose count soon after this. I'd been keeping tally marks in a journal, but once the number felt too big to really understand, I gave up.

There's no footage of me watching the news reports. Only memories. Only a letter I write to Minerva Krackle in purple crayon about how I believe her, about how nice it would be to see people like me in a movie, and thanks, I guess, for trying. At least that's the vibe I was going for in my letter, in pictures and words spelled the way I imagined they might be.

• • • • •

(1994) TIMELINE

The (second) Great Merlan performs a big splashy magic trick, as is the fashion with the most popular magicians. Her hair is long and black and wild, always curled around itself like fingers holding each other. She's been around since the 1970s but she looks younger than ever, that's what all the newscasters say, and we're putting a montage of them in this movie. A full minute of comments on her youth, her beauty, her tiny waist, and what was her diet routine anyway? They never ask about the first Great Merlan. He has taken care of that.

The (second) Great Merlan had been playing with water tank tricks over the last couple years, but for this trick she is dropping herself into the deepest tank of the Long Beach Aquarium, where she has asked for the addition of at least five new hungry sharks, just for good measure.

Before she is dropped into the tank, arms and legs chained together, a weight tied to her middle, she looks at the cameras and says to us, "You have been amazing. Remember that." And she falls.

The video of this trick is a multi-cam event, cutting from this angle to that angle, seeing The Great Merlan struggle for many minutes, as sharks circle closer and closer to her.

And then she is suddenly there, behind us—in the aquarium lobby, completely dry.

All cameras point to her and she bows.

"Thank you for your Time," she says.

• • • • •

(1989) VIDEO

The clip has the warm, slightly fuzzy quality of newsreels of the 1980s. Minerva Krackle, age forty-two, sits in a hotel room across from a woman with black hair and an Amazonian muscle structure, wearing a store-bought Wonder Woman outfit.

"Please repeat your name for the camera," says Krackle.

"Shelley," says the wondrous woman. Shelley fidgets in her chair and adjusts her costume. Her lips are tense and pulled thin. Krackle would later write that she smelled like lilies and that she would stare at something just over Krackle's shoulder, like a sea captain might at an approaching battleship in the distance.

"You don't have to wear that thing," says Krackle.

"I feel better in this," says Shelley.

"Okay."

"I'm not exactly comfortable with the real me. This is better. It's closer."

"Closer to what?" asks Krackle.

"Lots of people come talk to you, don't they?" asks Shelley. She pulls out a lasso and begins untying and retying the knots.

"There are certain kinds of people who are drawn to me, I guess," says Krackle. "Why did you reach out to me?"

"I don't know," says Shelley.

Shelley doesn't continue right away, so Krackle lets this hang in the air and walks across the room for some ice. For several minutes, the camera picks up Krackle over Shelley's shoulder, standing at the hotel room desk and dropping ice from the ice bucket into a coffee cup. With each drop, Krackle stares at the ice cube in the coffee, watching it melt, as Shelley, facing the camera, is intent on the lasso, tying and untying.

"There's this idea of heroes and villains," says Shelley. "I look like I'm a hero, I guess. Right? And I have these powers and I'm supposed to fight evil, right?"

Krackle drinks the now cold coffee and takes out her journal. She notes something down. "Do you have any powers?"

"I'm strong," says the wondrous woman.

"How strong?"

"Pretty strong. Stronger than those muscle guys on the TV."

"Anything else?"

"My sister was attacked," says Shelley. She swallows. "Raped. I tracked the guy down and killed him."

A pause, then: "Okay," says Krackle from across the room. This "okay" is heavier somehow, I think. The pause. The way the word falls down into Krackle's coffee the moment she says it.

"Was he evil?" asks Shelley. "Or am I evil because I killed him?"

"I haven't met anyone who is all evil," says Krackle.

"I haven't saved any cities or world leaders. I've just gotten revenge. If I were a hero, wouldn't I want to do something more?" Shelley has tied her lasso into a noose at this point. She looks up and straight into the camera. "Because I don't. Want to, that is."

Krackle walks back over and sits across from Shelley. Shelley seems to be waiting for another question, but Krackle offers nothing except a quiet sipping of coffee.

"What if I told you I made that all up?" says Shelley. "The rape and all that. I don't even have a sister. But I killed a guy all the same. Because I WANTED to?"

"Is that what you're telling me?" says Krackle.

Shelley shifts in her chair. She unties the noose and reties it. "I sometimes walk around Hollywood Boulevard with all those other guys dressed up like superheroes," she says. "Like, all the Disney characters and the comic book guys and the celebrity impersonators. People pay me to take pictures with them."

"Good money?" says Krackle.

"Good money? Seriously?" says Shelley. "How would I know? Those guys chased me outta there after a couple hours. Getting too close to their territory. There's some other chick who says she's Wonder Woman or something. Like she owns Wonder Woman."

"Okay," says Krackle.

"Okay," says Shelley, mocking. "Okay okay okay. I went back later and cut their throats, okay?"

"Is that true?" says Krackle.

"What's it matter?" says the wondrous woman. "Okay okay okay."

"You think you're evil?" asks Krackle. "In your letter to me, you used the word 'monster.' You think you're a monster?"

"Isn't that the word people use?" says Shelley.

"I've never liked it," says Krackle.

"I guess I don't know what that word means," says Shelley. "I was hoping you could tell me. You've interviewed enough of them."

"Depends on your point of view, I suppose," says Krackle.

"That's a cop-out," says the wondrous woman. "That's a load of horseshit."

In her journal, Minerva Krackle wrote that the price tag for the Wonder Woman costume was still hanging down Shelley's back. It had been marked down by sixty percent.

● ● ● ● ●

(1996) TIMELINE

An early web forum pops up; it anonymously tracks reports of "monsters" either found, on the run, and/or disappeared across the country.

The Sands Hotel and Casino is closed and demolished, along with all relics from The Great Merlan's long-running stage show.

• • • • •

(1997) VIDEO

The week of the release of *The Monsters Are Here!*, Minerva Krackle—age fifty—was booked to appear on three television shows and two local radio stations. But she made only one appearance on a local morning show called *Wake Up With Friends*. She did not yet know that the distribution company had done a secret final edit of her film.

Minerva Krackle is welcomed onto the show by the four hosts: Harvey, Ryan, Cindy, and Clare.

"I'm just so fascinated," says Clare, adjusting her silk poncho.

"Monsters! My god, how marvelous," says Harvey, loosening his red power tie.

"Thanks," says Krackle. She's smiling here. An unusual thing, but this feels like her moment, that's what the smile says to me. Krackle is about to be seen.

"But I just have to know," says Cindy, flipping her golden hair and smiling at the camera. "How did you get the idea for such a hilarious movie?"

"What?" says Krackle. And the smile is gone.

"How did you come up with all these pathetic characters?" says Clare. "You have quite an imagination!"

Krackle clears her throat. She manages to squeak out: "But it's all real."

Harvey and Ryan and Cindy and Clare are quiet for several seconds, then erupt into laughter.

"You are too MUCH!" says Harvey.

"Let's roll that footage," says Ryan, making a finger gun at an unseen producer.

The clip rolls. And Krackle sees part of her movie for the first time.

Swift cuts of John the werewolf, drunk and falling over in his seat. Shelley the wondrous woman trying to fly and falling off the hotel bed. Dr. Danger firing his Freeze Ray at the camera and sending sparks into his own face.

"It's just delightful," says Cindy.

"Fabulous," says Ryan.

"Quite a feat of comedic genius," says Clare.

"My kids will love it," says Harvey.

Krackle says nothing.

• • • • •

I'm recording an interview on my own because I feel like there's a hole here too. In my story, at least. In my story with Krackle.

I set the camera up in Krackle's living room, with the editing bay right behind me playing loops of footage already seen in the movie up until this point.

"I saw the movie when I was seven years old," I begin. "It was 1998. I wasn't allowed to watch a lot of movies then, but I'd heard about this movie. Kids at school really loved it."

Behind me, Krackle's interview pops on and plays in full, and you can hear the newscasters' voices cackling beneath my own.

"I went to the Blockbuster when I was like...ten...but I couldn't rent anything myself, of course, so I stole a copy. I stayed up late that night to watch it. I was a kid, but even I could tell that this was not the film she'd wanted to make. They'd added these graphics and jump cuts and wacky sound effects to make fun of everyone in the movie. Everyone Krackle had worked so hard to get to know, who had trusted her."

The clip you see in the movie is the sixth take. I had two panic attacks while recording this. I explain more, I go on and on describing what the wings feel like, what my childhood was like, how I've named all these new colors. But it's all too much. I cut it all out. I erase most of it. Almost all of it. I still want to go back and erase what I left in. Even now.

I lean into the camera, like Bennie had. For a little drama. "But what I saw was that I wasn't alone. I wondered if there were pieces of other kids buried in backyards or thrown in the dumpster. I wondered if it would ever stop."

I hold my gaze here, not knowing what I would put after this, but knowing I'd need the room. To make a clean cut.

• • • • •

(2019) VIDEO

Bobby Olsen—age seventy-five—slumps in his recliner, a velvet painting of a duck pond hanging on the wall behind him. I've hidden the stacks of newspapers, the conspiratorial headline cut-outs taped to his walls, the stacks of Chinese food takeout boxes rotting in the corner where Dr. Danger stands, silently, out of the frame, rubbing his nose to mask the smell of the apartment.

Bobby Olsen, the man who tried and failed to assassinate Minerva Krackle all those years ago, rubs his tongue over his teeth and stares at my back as I adjust a light. He gives only an occasional wary glance in Dr. Danger's direction.

"What's that on your back?" he asks.

I'm wearing my jean jacket with the holes, loose enough to cover my stumps.

"It's just a back brace. I got a thing with my back," I say.

"Let me see," says Bobby.

"It's not about me," I say. I'm sitting down near the camera now, checking my watch. I already feel like I've been here for hours.

"It's about Krackle," says Bobby. "You want to know why I tried killing the bitch."

"We can start there," I say. "Is that where you want to start?"

"I heard she up and disappeared," says Bobby. "Can't say I'm too weepy over that."

I let the silence in.

"Or do you think she's dead?" says Bobby. "That'd be a hoot."

"The police have no official announcement one way or the other," I say. We'd gotten another call earlier that day saying their leads had grown cold and they would have to take a step back from active investigating. In other words, they were giving up.

44

But this bastard didn't need to know that.

"She gets what she deserves, anyhow," says Bobby. "People always do. She was using this power of hers all wrong, you know. She shoulda been killing them all, not talking. Talking never got nobody nowhere."

"What power would that be?" I say. Play dumb. I learned that from Krackle.

Bobby licks his teeth again and burps a little deep in his throat. "She could see these things in the world. She could find them so easy. But what'd she do? Talk to them? Load of bullshit that," he says. "She shoulda been doing some good in the world."

"Did she interview you?" I say. "Is that why you feel so violent toward her?"

"I'm not a freak," says Bobby. "She never woulda been looking for me." He narrows his eyes. "But I came looking for her."

I'm getting that tightening in my chest when I want to punch someone. If you know what that sounds like, you can hear it in my voice.

"I'm just saying when you're given a gift, you should do some good in the world," says Bobby. "This world is bad enough as it is. Why you sitting by, letting the bad stuff go on. Pick up the damn baton and do your duty."

"And killing people was her duty?" I say. "Am I understanding? Just to clarify."

"Don't put words in my mouth," says Bobby. "That's one thing your boss never did, ya know. You could learn a thing or two."

"I'm just trying to understand," I say.

"What do ya want?" says Bobby. "You wanna know my sad story? You wanna know how I ended up this way?"

I say nothing.

"Yeah, didn't think so," says Bobby. "You just wantin' the story you wantin'. I'm a bad guy with a gun, that it?"

"You tried to murder her," I say.

"And I failed at that, didn't I?" says Bobby. "What a story."

"But why did you do it? " I say.

"Show me that 'back brace' of yours and maybe I'll tell ya," says Bobby.

Off camera, I'm moving my eyes toward the shotgun hanging on the wall. I'm wondering where the handguns are. I catch Dr. Danger's eye.

"Sometimes people do things and you ain't ever gonna know why, little girl," says Bobby. "Even if ya did, it wouldn't satisfy you, probably. Guess you got to live with that." Bobby snorts, leans in closer to the camera, looking me in the eyes. "You ain't willing to show me what you're hiding, why would I ever show you mine?"

Bobby laughs and laughs.

● ● ● ● ●

(2000) TIMELINE

The (second) Great Merlan is convicted of manslaughter after a water tank magic trick goes terribly wrong. Half of the very handsome male assistant ends up on top of the water tank, while his lower half sinks to the water below.

No one saw The Great Merlan, or the tank lid, or anything actually cut the man in half, but there he is all the same, during her penultimate trick of the evening back in Vegas, a trick she had performed literally thousands of times by this point.

Headlines called The Great Merlan mad. Insane. *Her brain is living in another time zone*. I scan each headline carefully and drop them into the movie edit.

● ● ● ● ●

(2001) VIDEO: FOUND FOOTAGE

A taped-at-home copy of *Wake Up With Friends* that includes an interview with Shelley the wondrous woman. I jump to the middle of the conversation because goddamnit, these shows are boring.

The same hosts are there: Harvey, Ryan, Cindy, and Clare.

"I'm just so fascinated," says Clare, adjusting her silk blouse.

"You really thought you were a monster?" says Harvey, smoothing his red power slacks.

"She'd convinced me I was special," says Shelley. She looks older and sadder without her knockoff Wonder Woman getup. "And I just wanted to believe it. I'd done terrible things. And I needed to know that I was the righteous one in the end. That woman, she really wants everyone to buy into her delusion of these creatures, just, *living among us*. Who *were* us. It's really very sad if you think about it, and I have *so much* sympathy for her."

"We had her on our show and she actually believed her movie was real. It was so sad!" says Harvey.

"But I just have to know," says Cindy, tucking her new blonde bob behind her ear. "Do you still have that Wonder Woman costume?"

"Oh I couldn't possibly fit into that thing" says Shelley. "I could barely fit into it *then*!"

They laugh and laugh.

"But really—what *did* you do anyway that was so *bad*," says Ryan, leaning his elbow onto the chair as if settling in for a cozy story.

"Oh *Ryan*! *You're* the bad one!" says Shelley. She's good at this. "You can read all about it in my memoir, *The Wonders of Being Wondrous*. Which is on bookshelves now."

"It's just delightful," says Cindy.

"Fabulous," says Ryan.

"Quite a feat of genius," says Clare.

"My wife will love it," says Harvey.

Shelley smiles and smiles.

● ● ● ● ●

(2019) VIDEO

A three-hour drive from the desert, the mummy feet and arms safely in the trunk, we finally reach Farris' Diner in Blue Jay, California. It is raining. Desert dust has turned to mud on the car, and you can barely hear the scraping and kicking of the mummy arms and feet in the trunk, what with the rain pounding against the roof.

I set up the camera for a shot of Liz the diner waitress and Minerva Krackle sitting across from each other in a booth against the front windows of the diner. Out the windows, you can see the main road and the edge of a deep forest on the other side. A drowning beehive trembles outside the door of the diner, and a pregnant woman is the only other patron in the place, sitting by herself in the farthest booth, slurping soup.

Liz the diner waitress pulls off her bright pink shoes and tosses them under the booth. Her waitress uniform is clingy and covered in coffee stains, but Liz wears it with a kind of class reserved for royalty.

"So, the feet and the arms," says Krackle.

"My sister Meggie was only twenty-three when she died," says Liz. "She wasn't real happy about it, or at least the part where she came *back* to life, so it's been hard to keep her under control. She had this real fascination with Egypt, you know, so my parents decided to bury her like a goddamn pharaoh—I mean, they put all her stuff around her in her coffin, her favorite things. I'm just glad they didn't kill me and bury me with her to be her guardian in the afterlife or something."

"You are kind of her guardian now though, aren't you?" asks Krackle.

Liz snorts and drinks her coffee.

"And then shortly after the funeral...Meggie woke up."

Krackle waits a moment, to see if Liz might offer some clue as to how this happened, but Liz is silent. "So many people have seen their lives change overnight since that first wave of...transformations. It must have been shocking."

Liz nods but is staring into her coffee. "I moved home. We lived together for a while. But it wasn't long until our moms couldn't handle it so they basically told me she was my problem now and they took off— haven't heard from them in some time. So years went by and we did okay but you know...sisters. Me and Meggie were getting on each other's nerves. We needed our own space. And she had started to smell... she was becoming more and more like a mummy. I had to wrap...gauze around parts of her to keep her together. So I build her this little tomb— out of one of those build-yourself sheds you get at the hardware store— and put all her favorite stuff in it and wire it so it's even got electricity. Electricity I pay for, by the way."

"Sounds like a nice setup," says Krackle.

"And I put a sign on it and everything so people think it's a mausoleum and maybe would have some respect. Problem is, people keep telling these ghost stories about hearing music in the woods and crying or something, and then they follow the sound and break in and steal her stuff. Someone made off with her stereo once—made her real mad. So she gets out and terrorizes people for a while until I can round her up. One time, I'd had it with the behavior so I took her feet off and put extra locks on her tomb door so she couldn't run off and no one else could get in."

"Why the desert?"

"I can't afford a plane ticket to the great pyramids, that's why."

"Okay," says Krackle, sipping the coffee she'd let go cold.

"But then someone got in again because those were cheap locks, stole her old pog collection and a Ricky Martin CD, and she got out again, crawled around on her hands, it was real disturbing. So that time I took her arms off."

"Seems extreme," I say from behind the camera.

Krackle glances at me, I can feel it, but I keep my gaze trained on Liz.

"I mean…cutting off a piece of someone just to keep her where she needs to be."

Liz looks me up and down. Something about that look makes me think she knows everything about me. "I didn't know what else to do," says Liz.

"You don't cut people up. That's what you don't do," I say.

"That's enough," says Krackle. She'd never broken an interview to scold me. I shut up immediately and Krackle turns back to Liz. "Tell me about the park and the suburbs."

"We lived in that house across the street for a while in middle school. I guess I thought pieces of Meggie might feel at home there."

I remember seeing the woman in the white nightgown, the one who had been watching as Krackle went into the park. She hadn't shown up on the video.

"So what does this have to do with that magician you used to work for?" says Krackle.

"I didn't work for her," says Liz. "I followed her around for a while. I was a fan."

"Okay." Krackle sighs.

"And I asked her for a spell to save Meggie," says Liz. "But when I met her…she was so out of her mind. She said she'd do it, but part of me

didn't believe she was capable. And Meggie died so of course I figured…
there it was. Proof. The Great Merlan was a fraud. Then, of course,
Meggie wakes up…but something is off."

"What kind of spell was this?" says Krackle.

"You ever heard of Time magic?" says Liz.

Krackle shakes her head. Liz looks around the diner, checks that no
one is listening.

"Time is a kind of curse," says Liz. "It's tangled all around Meggie
and there's nothing I can do about it."

"What are you saying?" says Krackle.

"I'm saying when you're about to lose someone you love very much,
the rules don't seem to apply to you," says Liz, clearing her throat and
putting her pink shoes back on.

"So you can't break Time magic?" says Krackle.

"Not in Meggie's case. If you find a way to untangle it, let me know,"
Liz says, pulling a rag from her apron. "Anyway, I'm sure you want to see
the tomb. Just let the arms and feet out and they'll lead the way."

"Come with us," says Krackle.

"Meggie doesn't want to see me. For years I'd go visit her, hoping
I'd show up and she would be dead. Just fell asleep and drifted off finally. But she never did. And she was so mad at me about the feet and the
arms…and one day I just couldn't find the tomb. I think Meggie figured
out how to manipulate something about the curse or Time that allows
her to hide from me."

"Can't say I blame her," I say.

Krackle whips her face around to me. "Stop."

"It's getting late. You don't want to be stuck out in the woods at
night when it's raining," says Liz.

"This might be a great time to make up with your sister. Come with
us."

Liz shakes her head. "If I'm there, you'll never find it. Now get
going. I got to clean up for the alcoholics. They got their AA meeting
here in an hour."

Krackle, Dr. Danger, and I wrap ourselves in rain gear. Outside, we
open the car trunk and the boxes. The feet and arms jump out, run across
the street without looking both ways, and disappear into the woods.

I do my best to keep the camera steady, but everything can't help but look like a low-budget horror movie.

• • • • •

(1993) VIDEO

There is a lot of Dr. Danger footage. We've gone around and around it, trying to find the moment that should be remembered. Dr. Danger likes the three hours during which he showed off each of his corsets and top hats and tailored pants and jackets, his puffy shirts and leather belts, his eyeglasses and monocles. A private fashion show during which Krackle asked very few questions.

I decided on this one. And I'm the one doing this edit, not him.

The film is dark and grainy, shot in such a way as to make Dr. Danger's recliner look taller, more angler, and generally more impressive. There is a fire burning behind him on a television screen. The TV antennae are bent toward the floor and the fire blinks in and out of existence every few seconds.

Krackle asks, "Do you have any ice?"

"Ice?" Dr. Danger crinkles up his nose.

"For the coffee."

"Why do you want ice for your coffee?"

"It's too hot," says Krackle.

"Isn't there a way to just make cold coffee?" asks Dr. Danger.

"I like to watch the ice melt," says Krackle. "The taste of melted ice is like nothing else."

Dr. Danger smirks and nods. He takes out his Freeze Ray, clicks it to its lowest setting, and points it at Krackle's coffee cup with a very, very slow pull on the trigger.

A single ice cube plops out of the gun and into Krackle's coffee.

Dr. Danger smiles. He so seldom smiles. But there it is.

Krackle writes very little in her journal about this interview, except that she is partial to the fedora with the purple feather, and that ice from a Freeze Ray gun makes her coffee taste like cinnamon.

• • • • •

This girl won't take no for an answer. She's been sending me letters and emails and packages for years now. Took me a while to realize the letter in the purple crayon was the same girl. I wasn't looking for an assistant. After what happened, I shouldn't trust anyone besides Dr. Danger.

But I indulged her and met up with her at Liz's diner—might as well get some work done while I was at it. I could bug Liz a bit more about the whole mummy rumor and I could see if this kid was dedicated enough to drive all the way out to Blue Jay to see me. And she does, the little weirdo.

But you know the real wild thing? She's got wings. Literally. She said she let them grow a little longer than normal just for this meeting. She's been cutting them off her whole life, but they always grow back—she just doesn't let them get to whatever size they want to be or can be or should be. I think they could be really large, really grand, if she'd just let them.

I ask her why she cuts them and she shrugs. They're not natural, she says. And I ask her what she means by natural and she says, you know, normal, and so I ask what she means by normal and she says the thing that keeps you invisible. And I tell her how there's lots of people I've met over the years that make their whole lives about being invisible and invisible isn't any easier than visible, it's not nicer or sweeter or anything like that. And she says that's why she wants to work for me. She wants to meet them.

I ask her why she wants to meet them. And she tells me it's the same reason as me, she suspects.

I just nod at her like I understand. But I don't. Because I don't know why I do this. I don't know why. I'm too old not to understand why.

So I hired an assistant.

$$\bullet \quad \bullet \quad \bullet \quad \bullet \quad \bullet$$

The night before I go to meet Liz again, probably for the last time, I am thinking about Bennie twirling his tentacle around my back, and I'm thinking about my parents holding me down in the tub that first time and all the other times—something I hadn't thought about in years, miraculously, except for this fucking movie, this stupid movie that Krackle ran out on and left on my doorstep to fix.

I can't sleep so I go out to the bar closest to Krackle's place, a little run-down dive that calls itself a pub but serves nachos and overcooked ramen on its late menu. I'm wearing the thinnest shirt I have and I tear off any remaining gauze before I head out. I can feel my stumps oozing through my shirt and into my jean jacket as I walk.

I bring my phone to record on, just in case. Not that I plan for this to be part of the movie. But it's a habit I've picked up from Krackle. You never know, do you, when the important moment might appear.

I drink for a long time in the darkest corner I can find. I record people as they pass by. Two hours of staring and whispering or ignoring completely, lost in their own haze of vodka and flirtation and that sinking feeling everyone gets in bars like this. A few can see blood seeping through the shoulder of my shirt and they ask me if I'm okay and I just nod and tell them to mind their business. Even when that's not what I want. It's not. Not even a little bit.

Then a scruffy-looking guy stumbles up to my table, half-drunk beer in hand, and leans in close, staring at my shoulder where the ooze has really started to make itself known, and he says, "Do you need... something?"

"That's a weird question," I say.

"That's the vibe, man," he says. "Like you need help."

I laugh long and hard into my empty glass.

"So do you? Need something? Like a drink? Or a...doctor?"

I shake my head. "You wanna see something?" I say. I think it's sexy, the way I say it, but when watching back, no. Not at all.

But he nods anyway and climbs onto the chair beside me and I turn my back to him, which now is soaked with the ooze.

I start to lift my shirt so he can really get a good look and he helps me, and then there they are, the stumps, growing back already, and raw, teeny tiny feathers are starting to sprout along the edges, the fuzzy kind, like baby birds have.

"Whoa," he says.

"You can touch them," I say.

And he does. Gently at first, and then he's swirling his fingers around the swollen wings, and I let him. It hurts and it feels good and it's all I wanted, really. But how do you ask for this? How do you ask anybody for this?

Anyway.

It's all on video. All of it.

I don't know if this will be in the movie.

When I leave the bar, I have a message from Dr. Danger. The police were able to recover some of the footage from the camera in the tomb and *where the fuck are you anyway, get back to work, you lazyass.*

● ● ● ● ●

(1994) VIDEO

A fedora hat floats in the middle of a dance studio. A mirror wall reflects back Minerva Krackle, age forty-seven, as she walks around the fedora.

"No strings, no illusions," she's saying.

"The amazing invisible woman," says a voice. A cackle erupts from beneath the fedora and echoes around the studio.

"Why did you want to meet here today?" asks Krackle, in that voice she uses when she knows the answer already.

"I was a dancer before this happened," says the voice from under the fedora.

"State your name for the camera," says Krackle.

"Isabel Martinez. You may have heard of me." She giggles.

Krackle checks her notes. "Five years with Parsons Dance Company. Another four with Alvin Ailey."

"I have a great new piece that I think could really reach people," says Isabel. "Maybe they won't notice how I'm, you know, *the way I am.*"

"You're hoping they won't notice that you're invisible?" asks Krackle.

"You can convince people of almost anything," says Isabel. "If you try hard enough."

"How do you choreograph something when you can't see yourself?"

"Eventually you get to know your body so well you don't need to see it. No need for mirrors. It's just like if I went blind. It would be the same."

"Can you give me a preview of your piece?"

Isabel breathes a deep, happy breath. The fedora goes flying across the room. The stamping of feet across the floor. Music switches on. A piece of silk lifts up from a chair in the corner and floats in front of the mirror. To the rhythm of the music, the silk twists around an invisible body—shaped, then shapeless, and so on. Through three minutes, Krackle makes no notes in her journal.

When the music ends, the silk falls motionless to the ground. There is silence.

"That was beautiful," says Krackle.

Isabel says nothing. A bucket floats up from the corner and comes closer to Krackle.

"It's different when you can see all the movements. Let me show you," says Isabel, dumping the bucket over, spilling a thick layer of pink powder on her invisible body, powder that clings to every crevice of her muscles. Her empty eye sockets stare out at Krackle. "Watch."

Isabel dances with the silk once more and Krackle watches her. With each move, each bead of sweat, the pink powder slowly flakes off.

At the end of the song, the powder covers the floor, and Isabel is invisible once again.

Krackle is off-screen, but in the silence that follows Isabel's final moves, one, sharp intake of breath can be heard, and a muffled cry.

"You get it?" Isabel asks.

● ● ● ● ●

(2007) TIMELINE

The (second) Great Merlan is out of jail but nowhere to be seen. A (third) Great Merlan has taken her place. She's younger, blonder, but very dedicated to recreating the (second) Great Merlan's every move. She's a traditionalist. She follows the magic.

Krackle is the only one who really notices this. The news programs proclaim that it's great having The Great Merlan back on stage, that she hasn't aged a day, that she's better than ever.

There are new internet forums tracking cases of the curious monster syndrome, the mass hysteria event that no one acknowledges, that we're not allowed to speak about in public. Krackle follows them all.

She's worried that she might need to pick up the work again. She has a feeling she's seen this all before, and it doesn't end well for her.

Or maybe it does.

• • • • •

(2015) VIDEO

This clip is shadowy and at an odd angle. We're on the casino floor of the Golden Nugget in old-town Las Vegas and not technically legally allowed to take video, but the Frankenstein casino girl won't be off work until 2 a.m. and we have to be on the road by midnight.

So we're idling by slot machines in the darkest corner, the camera wrapped in a sweatshirt and balanced on my lap as Dr. Danger circles us, keeping an eye out and occasionally sticking a quarter into a slot.

The Frankenstein casino girl is giggling. She is slender and her shoulders droop down to her right side. There are stitches around every crease and bend of her body. The paleness of her torso changes sharply to the deeper tan of her face right at the middle of her neck; her left arm is bulkier and more weathered than the dark smooth skin of her right; one skinny white leg crosses over a wooden one. A tray of cheap drinks sits on the stool beside her.

"Effie," says Krackle, "Forgive me the question, but are you technically dead?"

Effie the Frankenstein casino girl giggles again. "No, got a heart that's beatin' and everything. It's a bit oversized, so won't last as long's yours, so they tell me, but it's beatin' all right."

"So when did this start?"

"Oh, I had to be two at the least. Pieces just started falling off of me. First a leg, then an arm. They said I died once and they had to bring me back."

"How did they do that?"

"Shot me with some jumper cables attached to the Volvo and I started gigglin' like a crazy bird. You know that e.e. cummings poem: 'here is little Effie's head / whose brains are made of gingerbread / when the judgment day comes / God will find six crumbs / stooping by the coffinlid

/ waiting for something to rise / as the other somethings did / you imagine His surprise." Effie slaps her knee. "Oh lord, that's me. Only got six crumbs left."

"How long have you been in Vegas?" asks Krackle.

Effie drinks down one of the cocktails on the tray.

"I thought you didn't want to talk about that, ma'am."

"Only asking how you landed here," says Krackle, gently.

"Everyone got their special kind of peculiars," says Effie. "I don't want to talk about it."

"Okay," says Krackle.

"You know how much someone will pay just to see the top part of me? Just to use one of the arms, in, you know, in whatever way they want?"

"No," says Krackle.

"A lot," says Effie.

"Okay," says Krackle.

"But I'm not that girl," says Effie, picking up another cocktail. "Just 'cause a girl's made of bits and pieces and crumbs, don't mean those bits and pieces and crumbs are for sale."

Dr. Danger screams out. He's won ten dollars in quarters.

●　●　●　●　●

(2019) VIDEO

The feet and arms lead Krackle, Dr. Danger, and me to a storage shed covered in vines and leaves in a small glade, its roof coming to a sharp point like a pyramid, about two miles into the forest. There is an inscription in the rock with Meggie's name and birth and death dates. The feet and arms circle the pyramid-shed like excited dogs, knocking against the structure, sending leaves flying off the vines. They find the opening and disappear inside.

Minerva Krackle finds the opening as well and sticks her head in.

"Hello, Meggie," she says, her voice muffled by the tomb. "Your sister Liz sent us out here to return your limbs. Would you mind doing an interview?"

By the time this clip starts, the mummy girl, Meggie, has reattached her arms and feet. She has cleaned up her tomb slightly to fit Krackle, Dr. Danger, the camera, and me into the small space.

The walls are covered with band posters from the late 1990s. Piles of pogs (returned by the thief), snap bracelets, bags of Skittles and microwave popcorn, photos of family, a bag of makeup, and slim, clingy dresses on hangers. Meggie's bandages are covered in glitter and bedazzled with rhinestones, her gray, rotting skin complementing the cold glint of it all. She smiles at the camera with only three teeth, her breath coming out in black clouds of dust that settle on the ceiling.

"You have a kind face," Meggie the Mummy says to Krackle.

"So do you," says Krackle.

Meggie giggles.

"Liz says you weren't happy being dead," says Krackle.

"I didn't care much either way," says Meggie. "I got more attention when I was dying, I'll say that. I had a cancer scare twice—imagine that! The first time went away and then it came back and that was that. And then when I was dead, boy, the attention! No one ever brought me presents before. Look." Meggie picks up an old collage of magazine cut-outs pasted to fading construction paper. The cut-outs are of beautiful women from advertisements, celebrities from the '90s and early 2000s, models from Paris. In Sharpie, someone had written: *Meggie, always beautiful.*

"No one ever said that when I was alive," she says

"Maybe they're afraid of Time," I say, behind the camera.

Meggie's face drops. A piece of gray skin flakes off her cheek and into her lap. "There's no such thing," she says.

"As Time?" I say.

"When Time has been wrapped around you and kept you in one place for so long, then you can talk to me about whether or not it exists," says Meggie. "Who's this chick?"

"She's my assistant," says Krackle. "And that's Dr. Danger, my guardian."

Dr. Danger takes off his top hat and bows.

"So you, like, interview monsters?" says Meggie the Mummy.

"All sorts," says Krackle. "But I'm not keen on that name."

"Are they all real? Like, really real monsters?" Meggie folds the construction paper collage and stores it carefully away.

"I'll say yes," says Krackle. "They are people. Real just like you."

"Do you think of yourself as a monster?" I ask.

I've watched this clip over and over and can't remember why I asked this question. I tried to never interrupt interviews, but something about this trip made me jumpy.

If I'd just stayed quiet, maybe Krackle would still be here.

Meggie jabs a look in my direction. "My *sister* is a monster. She tried to keep me here. Tried to get me to die, but she was the one who was so sad about me dying in the first place. And our *moms*! Where the hell did they go anyway? Monsters!"

"I'm sure they loved you very much," says Krackle.

"I'm hungry," Meggie says suddenly. "I can't keep going unless I eat."

"Would you like some pancakes? How's blueberry?" asks Krackle.

Meggie smiles with her three teeth. "Liz makes the best ones." Her smile fades immediately, catching herself evoking her sister. "But I don't want *her* here. Just the pancakes."

Krackle turns to Dr. Danger and me. "Go grab some pancakes from the diner for Meggie. Leave the camera."

I change out the memory card, tucking away our road trip footage into my camera bag and putting a fresh one in the camera we leave in the tomb. Krackle can talk with Meggie as long as she wants. I grab my backup camera and switch it on for our pancake side quest.

We don't protest—we know that will not go over well with Krackle. But Dr. Danger frowns as soon as we exit the tomb.

The footage of the walk back to the diner is dark and wet and very, very quiet. Dr. Danger walks behind me by a few steps the whole way, and I find myself glancing back at him every minute or two, fully expecting a knife or Freeze Ray gun lodged into my spine any second.

Liz puts in an order of blueberry pancakes to go. We don't tell her it's for her sister. There's no opportunity to do so privately because the

AA meeting is still in full swing, and the pregnant woman is still there, lying in one of the booths, staring at her reflection in the napkin holder.

The walk back to the tomb is longer and wetter and darker. Dr. Danger's top hat slumps from the weight of the water.

I have a sinking feeling the whole time. It is the same feeling I had when watching the news footage of Minerva Krackle being shot by Bobby Olsen. My back is hurting because I haven't had a chance to trim lately, and those lumps of flesh on my back are no longer lumps of flesh, and I can barely hide them beneath my jacket. Dr. Danger keeps looking at the lump in my jacket out of the corner of his eye.

And when we reach the glade again, Krackle is gone and Meggie is dead. Actually dead, arms folded across her chest. Two candles are lit on either side of her, and her stereo plays Joan Jett's album *I Love Rock & Roll* on repeat. Where Krackle was sitting, there are just a few drops of blood, as if in suspended animation on the blanketed floor.

The camera we left in the tomb has stopped filming and appears waterlogged, though the air inside the tomb is dry. A stack of Krackle's journals and a hard drive with footage are beside the camera. And there is a simple note, in Krackle's handwriting, addressed to Dr. Danger and me. A goodbye note.

I try to play back the footage on the camera, but it is jammed and unruly and corrupted. We both read the note. I am shaking but I keep filming on my backup camera.

"I don't understand. Where did she go?" I ask the tomb, the mummy, Dr. Danger. "Krackle?!" I call.

Dr. Danger points his Freeze Ray at me, only a few inches from my nose. "What's under your jacket?" he says.

"What?" I'm shaking because of the cold and the dead body a few feet away that was just a laughing young woman an hour before, and I'm feeling completely and absolutely alone.

Dr. Danger grabs the camera and turns it on me. "What's under your jacket? There are big lumps on your back. Are they some kind of weapon? Did you disintegrate her?"

I shake my head. I asked Krackle years ago, when we first met, to not tell anyone about the wings, about me. I figured she must have told Dr. Danger at some point and he'd just been quiet about it. Dr. Danger and

I never talked. Not really.

But she kept her word. She never told anyone.

"Show me. Show me you don't have a weapon."

There are tears in my eyes that I'm trying to hold back. This is on tape. You can see the tears hovering there. "Is she dead? Do you think she's dead? Why would she just leave?" I say.

"Show me."

"I don't have a weapon."

"Show me." He clicks his Freeze Ray to the highest setting and yanks my backup camera out of my hands and points it at me. "Now," he says.

In the mummy's tomb and now on camera, I take off my jacket and stretch out my stubbly wings, the ones I've recently cut off, which are growing back as I watch this again.

It hurts to stretch them out, and you can see this on my face on the tape. Even when the wings are grown out a bit more, I keep them folded and tucked and inert for so long, I almost don't have the muscle to let them take up space in the room.

"Why haven't I seen these?" says Dr. Danger, keeping his Freeze Ray firm at my nose.

"I trim them. I don't usually let them get this big, but I've been…" I look around the room. "Distracted."

"Are you hiding guns? Is that feather a bomb?" Dr. Danger yanks a feather off my left wing and I yelp. He holds the feather up to the camera for a closer inspection.

I feel dizzy. I slump to the floor of the tomb and Dr. Danger follows me with the camera.

"Why are you crying?"

"I'm not," I say, clearly crying.

"You're trying to trick me," he says.

"It hurts," I say. I point to my wings. I'm trying to let them relax but I can feel the skin of my back bleeding and cracking.

"Have some pride," Dr. Danger says. He throws a bit of mummy bandage at me and I dab at my eyes before realizing what it is.

"Gross," I say.

"How 'bout you use those wings of yours to fly around, try to spot

Krackle from above? We can see where she went."

"I can't," I say.

Dr. Danger pushes a button on his Freeze Ray that makes the thing hum in high-pitched electricity. "How about you try," he says.

Outside the tomb, the rain has slowed down to barely a mist. I'm standing in the clearing, Dr. Danger behind the camera. Blood has soaked the back of my shirt. I stretch out the little bits of wings I have and the effort splits my skin even more. I hold back a scream, because fuck Dr. Danger for this.

I try to fly but it's impossible. The wings aren't fully grown. The skin is raw. And I've literally never done this before. I get a foot off the ground and crash.

The pain of wings trying to fly for the first time is a kind of pressurized tearing of the muscles. Pressure as if my brain and lungs are going to explode any second out of their cavities. Tearing like each tiny, individual muscle fiber is being sliced open with dull scissors.

The pain and the rain show me new colors I don't name.

One. Two. Three times. *Crash, crash, crash.*

After the last crash, I pick myself up in a surge of anger. I push past Dr. Danger, disappear back into the tomb for a moment and reemerge with my jean jacket, pulling a Swiss Army knife from its inside pocket.

Kneeling in the mud, in direct line of the camera, I slowly cut my wings off. Piece by piece. Letting the bloody chunks fall around me and sink into the soil.

But Dr. Danger is in shock and he lets the camera go wonky, so you can't see everything I'm doing here. It's why I later do the bathroom shoot.

I could blame him, but I would have been doing it anyway.

By the end, I'm out of breath and my shirt is soaked in red and rainwater and sweat. I've never done this outside before, never in the rain, never in front of anyone else except for Krackle. The moment I could handle a knife myself, I locked my parents out of the bathroom every week. This was my body. I'd do it my way.

I collapse into the mud and stay there, hunched, knees sinking into the earth, my back exposed, skin begging for each cool drop of rain that finds its way to me. The wind quietly picks up the loose feathers around me and carries them off into the trees.

Dr. Danger leaves the camera on its tripod and walks over to me. He points his Freeze Ray at my back and slowly pulls the trigger.

Two large ice cubes fall from the gun and drop onto the wounds. The cold numbs me and my breathing relaxes.

It smells like cinnamon.

"Turn that damn camera off," I say.

• • • • •

(2019) VIDEO

It's dark in Krackle's living room. Maybe about 1:30 a.m., based on the brightness of the streetlamps I can see through the window behind her. Krackle once complained about the streetlamps being too bright through her bedroom window, but instead of just buying her some black-out curtains, Dr. Danger scaled the poles and hooked up timers to dim the streetlamps to a more reasonable glow. The dimming always began at 1:45 a.m., when Krackle usually made her way to bed. In this video, the lamps are still their brightest, whitest light.

It's the night before we left on the road trip, before Krackle met Meggie the Mummy. I'm upstairs on a futon sleeping, and Dr. Danger is curled on a camping pad in the hall outside Krackle's bedroom.

The clip starts suddenly, with static and out of focus, as if it is an un-expected signal interrupting this evening's regularly scheduled program. Which it is. Because this clip had been lurking on its own hidden piece of the timeline, where Krackle thought I'd never find it. Or where she knew I'd find it, if I were actually paying attention to what she'd already laid out for me. It had been nothing more than a quick blip, the fastest black bar of nothingness near where Krackle's edit had ended and mine began. A strange artifact that had a trail.

Krackle is looking into the camera, during the earliest hour of the day of her disappearance. And she's talking to me.

"Harper, you've probably guessed by now how I want this movie to end," Krackle says. "It's what I've wanted for you from the day I met you. But it's not my story to tell. This is your choice, in the end. Cut yourself out if you'd like. I know you know how.

"I've always had a kind of antagonistic relationship with Time. I could never keep track of it, and I've tried to capture it all my life. Time runs away from us. Because we are always wasting it, or crunching it, or killing it.

"Before I made my first film, I started to see how it moved. Normally, Time stretches us over our whole lives, pulls at us, pinches us, shapes away all the bullshit until we are whittled down to our true form. We like to blame Time for this, but it's a collaboration. There is so much we choose in the process, so much shaped by our desires and fears, and so much warped by the things the world tells us has value.

"But Time has been swirled about recently. And it's taken us with it.

"The Great Merlan has this incantation she does in her shows. I'd never thought much about it until recently. *Time is shapeless. It cannot be moved or traveled. It can only be rearranged.*

"Time shows us who we are eventually. Time takes us where we need to go. But it rearranges us in the process.

"Remember that it's the monster you can't see that is the scariest. Because it lives in your imagination. Because we'll always create our own hell, our own private beast to gnaw at our insides. And then pretend like it's just another Tuesday."

Krackle smiles and then looks just above the camera, as if something is floating there, putting on a show for her. The streetlamps start to dim behind her. She's quiet enough that I can hear the *drip drip drip* of the leak in the ceiling.

"I love this part," she says, lost in whatever she's watching.

The clip ends there.

● ● ● ● ●

(2019) VIDEO

I hurry home after being felt up at the bar and Dr. Danger is there, footage queued up, not wanting to watch it without me. I think he's actually scared to watch it without me, but I decide not to tease him about that just at this moment.

We press play. The video is garbled like an old VHS tape that has been left out in the rain. Krackle and Meggie sound a little like they are underwater. But there she is. There they are.

In the video, while Dr. Danger and I are walking back to the diner to get pancakes, Meggie and Krackle talk for quite a while, discussing where Meggie traveled and where she'd always wanted to go, what it felt like to die, her favorite bands, and so on. Meggie tells Krackle about her curse.

"It didn't start out as a curse," says Meggie. "But I think many curses don't start out that way. They evolve into curses, and those are harder to get rid of."

"So what did it start out as?" asks Krackle.

"My sister was trying to save me," she says. "She was a great magician. Like, a real one. She took a piece of Time and wrapped it around me, wrapped me like a mummy. You can see it if you concentrate." She holds her arm up for Krackle to look. "Concentrate on my arm. You'll see it."

"I don't see anything yet," says Krackle.

"Keep looking," says Meggie. "Liz wrapped my Time around me so it would tangle up and not move forward and just sorta keep me here. 'Cept she did it when I'd already died and there's some things that don't get fixed up after death, you know? I think she thought I'd stay the same, but no one stays the same, right?"

"I've been studying this a long time," says Krackle. "And I think The Great Merlan, the original one, something about his Time magic affected a lot of people. It turned people inside out."

"Long before I died, she used it on me," says Meggie. "When the cancer came. The magic, like, put a pause on my insides. I was paused for a long Time."

"And it killed you?" said Krackle.

"No, the cancer did, silly," says Meggie. "But Liz needed me. She kept tangling up the Time around me."

"I don't understand," says Krackle. "*Liz* did this? I thought it was—"

"Can't you see it?" says Meggie. "It's everywhere. You of all people have to see it!"

"I still don't see anything," says Krackle.

"Keep looking. It looks like a cloud."

"A cloud?" Krackle looks up above the frame of the camera. Meggie follows her gaze. As they watch, something seems to move above their heads. They are more shrouded in shadow than before.

"Where'd that come from?" says Meggie.

"It's been following me around my whole life," says Krackle. "Never knew what it was until now."

"So you *can* see it," says Meggie.

"I see your wraps. I see them now," says Krackle, running her hand up and down Meggie's arm. "Someone really must have loved you to do all this."

Meggie is quiet for a moment. "I guess so. I mean, I know." Meggie looks up at Krackle and seems to have tears in her eyes, but it is hard to tell from the video quality. And I'm unsure if mummies are even able to cry.

Krackle holds Meggie's mummy hand with the stubbed fingers. "Maybe we can loosen the wraps a bit now? What do you think? Since we can see them so clearly."

"You do mine and I'll do yours" says Meggie.

Meggie looks up at the cloud and back at Krackle, and smiles with her last three teeth.

The video warps a bit here and we lose several minutes inside the tomb.

But when the video pops in again, Krackle's cloud bursts open and it begins to rain. But the rain is not water or any liquid you can recognize. I've watched this clip over and over. I've zoomed in on the rain, frozen the video at just the right moment. I've stared into the droplets of this no-rain, and all I can say is that it is like many movies on fast forward, layered on top of each other, and if I could smell the rain through the monitor—I'd say it smelled of subway trains and cinnamon and the desert and salt water dripping through the ceiling and the iron in the blood soaking through my shirt.

Krackle and Meggie open their mouths and let the rain fall in. As the rain falls, Krackle and Meggie are shifting out of focus, bleeding into each other, as if something is unwrapping itself around each of them. Krackle picks up a notebook and begins to write a note to Dr. Danger and me. She tells me to finish the movie. She tells Dr. Danger to be good.

As she finishes writing, you can barely make out her limbs anymore.

She's dissolving, floating away. Piece by piece until she's disappeared from the video completely.

The camera runs for a great while longer, recording a room with only the dead body of Meggie and the sound of rain. And then it slowly screeches into nothingness.

● ● ● ● ●

(2019) VIDEO

When Dr. Danger and I pull up for the final time in front of Farris' Diner, the front window has been smashed in, branches of a now-removed tree still lying on the front walkway. A large piece of cardboard has been taped over the hole, and in the opposite corner the AA group is talking in low murmurs. They look up at us when we enter with a jingle of the door. Dr. Danger gets all of this on tape.

"She's out back," says one of the guys in a flannel shirt. His voice is sugary. "Hey Harry. They're here."

A gruff-looking line-cook that vaguely looks like the fun uncle character from one of those sitcoms I watched as a kid pokes his head out of the kitchen door, nods for us to follow him, and then disappears.

We follow Harry to the damp backyard of Farris' Diner, where he leaves us with Liz, who is leaning against the dumpster, smoking a cigarette.

"I hear those things will kill you," I say.

"Weird," says Liz. She nods to the camera. "Already recording, I see?"

"Don't mind, do you?" I say.

Liz shrugs and drags on her cigarette. Deep circles are etched under her eyes and it seems as if Liz hasn't slept in days. I can smell the sweat and pancake syrup in Liz's shirt, even through the cloud of smoke. Even through the stench of wet earth.

Liz looks at Dr. Danger. "How's the Freeze Ray holding up?"

"Whatever you did, it's working like new," he says.

I glare at him. He never told me he'd been talking to Liz. Maybe I'm a little jealous. But he should have told me. We're partners now, whether he likes it or not.

Time to take control.

"What happened to the window?" I say.

"A tree blew through it. Wind was something terrible yesterday," says Liz.

I let the silence settle between us. I watched Krackle do this hundreds of times, letting space urge people to speak. Usually, if Krackle was in the room, they wanted to speak. They were going to do so no matter the question.

Liz doesn't speak. She just smokes and watches me. Her stare makes me uncomfortable, as if she is seeing things I could never hope to see. She flicks something away in the air in front of me. Then again. A bug, I guess, but I didn't see anything there. I try to keep myself from fidgeting while Liz smokes and smokes until the cigarette burns almost down to her finger.

And then: "Are you The Great Merlan?" I ask.

Liz smiles. "Who?" she says.

"You know who," I say.

"You're not great at this interview thing," says Liz.

"She's really not," says Dr. Danger.

"The Great Merlan was a stage magician. Died several years ago on stage in the middle of her act," I say.

"Then I suppose I'm not her," says Liz, blowing an impossible ring of smoke in my face. This isn't on the video of course, but it smells like chlorine, not like smoke. I'm going to note this in my journal later. Because after all this, I will start a journal.

I'd been to a show or two of The Great Merlan's. Had actually been at the show where The Great Merlan died. I'd gotten a VIP pass that night. Had even hoped that The Great Merlan could help me with my condition. Back when I believed in magic. None of this is on the tape, of course. It may not make it into the movie.

Liz looks at me, at the camera, with a new kind of light in her eyes. She smiles. "You a fan of this…what was the name? The Great Merlan?"

"I was. Yes," I say.

"Was," says Liz, almost as if it hurts her. "So, you like magic? Like coin tricks and shit?" Liz steps close to me until she is only inches from my nose.

Still, even this close I cannot smell smoke.

"I personally think magic is stupid," says Dr. Danger.

"You're a smart man," says Liz.

"The Great Merlan was more than just coin tricks," I try to say but stammer a bit.

Liz smiles. "Watch this."

Liz places her fingers behind my left ear. Something tickles my neck, but I keep still, trying to ignore the quickening in my chest.

Liz pulls her hand back, revealing a quarter. "How do ya like that?"

"So you have heard of her?" I say.

Liz frowns. "Meggie used to love that one," she says.

"I'll take that for a yes?"

Liz turns away and I already miss her closeness. Once a fan, always a fan. Even when our heroes become problematic. She flicks some things in the air around her.

"I was her apprentice for a while," says Liz. "Before that, I followed her around for a long time. A groupie of sorts. Back when I was a different person. Learned a few things."

"Okay," I say, remembering a few Krackle-isms.

"I was a very different person," says Liz.

"Sure," I say.

"I know what you're doing," says Liz.

"Have you been out to the tomb since Krackle disappeared?"

"Why would I? It's a tomb. She's in her tomb." Liz swallows, looks away from me. "What more is there to do? I've held a funeral for her in my head every day since the first diagnosis."

"We can go out there with you. Tonight," I say.

"Fuck off," says Liz.

"Stop beating around the bush," says Dr. Danger.

"Are you or have you ever been The Great Merlan?" I say.

"You watched the clip you sent me, yeah?" says Liz, crossing her arm over her body, getting stiff and defensive. "The one with Meggie and Minerva?"

"I watched them both die," I say.

"That's not what happened," says Liz. "It was something else. A release. I guess. Something I couldn't do. Something The Great Merlan couldn't do."

"Too bad the magician is dead," I say. "Maybe The Great Merlan knew more than you think she did."

"No. I don't think so," says Liz.

"I'm going to ask you one more time," I say.

"You're really *really* bad at this," says Liz.

Dr. Danger shrugs like he can't disagree.

I pause. Time for a new angle. "It's too bad she died in the water chamber. I always thought that was so strange. Of all the people who might accidentally drown...you'd think she would have the power to save herself," I say.

"No one does," says Liz.

I let this hang in the air. I stare at Liz, then let my gaze soften out toward the woods. I'm becoming more and more comfortable with silences.

Liz fidgets. "What does it matter?" she says. "Why does it matter who I was?"

"Because sometimes we try to cut off parts of ourselves and they grow back," I say, keeping my gaze locked on a particular tree with a protruding knot about six feet off the ground. It looks like my own stumps—even a bit painful like them too. "No matter what we do."

Liz steps closer to me again, but this time I'm prepared. I steady my breath and cross my arms. Then I uncross them because I remember something Krackle said about body language—about being open to whatever the interviewee was going to offer, to not close them off before they had a chance to speak.

"What did you cut off?" says Liz.

Dr. Danger snorts and I throw him a glare.

"Are you the Great Merlan?" I say, looking finally back at Liz. "Are you the famous magician who faked her own death? Who lost control of the magic that saved her sister? Who has locked herself away in a little café for so long that she's probably affecting the weather?" I hold my breath. The weather thing was a shot in the dark, but I'd noticed the odd weather patterns in Blue Jay, since Krackle started talking about Liz, since I started doing research about the diner, and since I started to trace certain patterns in the world wherever Liz seemed to move.

Liz sticks the stub of her dead cigarette in her pocket and uses both hands to flick the air around me. It's annoying more than anything. But she's mumbling something.

And suddenly I can feel my wings growing and growing—faster than they have ever grown before. Liz is staring at me, mumbling, flicking the air, and as she speeds up, so does the growing. I take off my jacket before they can rip through—my T-shirt is already a goner. They grow and grow until I fall to my knees under their weight, as they stretch out up to the sky, towering above my head, until they are full and wide and so strong. And they don't hurt one bit. None of it does.

Liz steps back and stares at the wings. "Ah. I see," she says. "You cut these off."

"What did you do?" I ask, trying not to panic, hands clinging to the earth and chunks of asphalt I'm crouching on, trying to steady myself, but all I can think about is how long it's going to take to remove them at this size.

"It's just an illusion," Liz says, reaching out and plucking a feather from my right wing. That one stings. "Best to think of it as just an illusion."

"Doesn't feel like an illusion," I say, standing up slowly, finding a new balance.

She holds the feather up to the light and I can see all kinds of colors there. Gordon and Isabela and Henrietta.

I stumble a bit, but Liz and Dr. Danger keep me from falling. Liz hands me the feather, which I take and hold with both hands as if it will break if I drop it.

She flicks her fingers in the air again and the wings are gone, down to the stubs they were just a minute before.

But the feather remains in my hand.

"Does that answer your question?" Liz smiles. "I still keep up the basic skills. I just don't want to mess it all up again." She removes the cigarette stub from her pocket and blows onto it. Within her breath is all the smoke and ash and paper she's just inhaled, swirled together like a mini storm cloud, a hurricane, circling together until the cigarette pieces itself back together. I'm holding my own breath, so I can't quite tell you what it smells like. But the smell wouldn't be on the video anyway.

Liz looks over the new patched-up cigarette and tucks it into her apron. "Haven't given a dime to Big Tobacco in almost a decade," she says.

● ● ● ● ●

Liz tells me what it was like when she decided to bring her sister back. She was busy on tour, had missed her mothers' voicemails, had missed the wake and the funeral. She only had a few moments to sit alone with Meggie's body before the closing of the casket. And she saw it: a million pieces spread out before her, all of Meggie's Time that she ever, and never, used.

Time looks different for the dead.

It took a while, but Liz managed to pick out an odd-shaped piece— one that was perhaps out of a dream; warm, easily stretched and molded like clay—and she wrapped that Time around the body that both was and wasn't her sister. She wrapped her in a loop of her own Time. Liz said the incantation that the witches taught her during her secret training as she was preparing to take over as the (third) Great Merlan. The words they told her never to use. Because when the (first) Great Merlan ignored them, disaster followed.

But Meggie sat up. And Liz forgot all about that.

Liz called her publicist. Her manager. Canceled The Great Merlan's tour—all except one date.

Liz as The Great Merlan does the tank trick. But this time she lets herself drown.

"Goodbye," she says to the audience. "You have been amazing. Remember that." And into the water she goes.

There is clear archival footage of this trick, and I put my favorite parts into the movie. Liz as The Great Merlan struggling in the water. I shouldn't be surprised she can pull off a fake death, but I'm impressed every time I watch it.

The headlines read *The Great Merlan Dies in Agony—Live On Stage!*

The original The Great Merlan gets royalties for this. For all of it.

And then Liz is just Liz again. And The Great Merlan is dead.

• • • • •

(2019) VIDEO + AUDIO

It's after midnight, two days before the due date for the movie, and Dr. Danger and I break into the house in Murrieta, across from the park where they found the mummy arms. I start recording before we even leave the car, so the recording is full of heavy breathing, walking, wind, the breaking of glass.

We settle in an upstairs bedroom, near the window where I saw the ghost to begin with. The house has been empty for several years, a product of foreclosure and prices too high for the area. It's a tract home, just like all the homes on the block, and I feel, as we walk up the stairs, vaguely like we're walking through ten houses at once, that the whole block of homes is made of mirrors, reflecting each other on and on into infinity.

I say as much out loud.

"Shut up, won't you," says Dr. Danger. "You'll scare the ghost away."

"Ghosts," I correct him.

In the bedroom, the recording is dark and gray, lit mostly from the streetlights through the window and Dr. Danger's flashlight. I set up the Ouija board despite Dr. Danger's worries. We light a candle and do a few rituals the internet suggested to welcome the spirits.

"What is it like on the other side?" I ask as a warm-up question.

The room is silent, but on the audio recording you can faintly hear the word *dull* being repeated by a faraway woman's voice.

"I'm not sure why this needs to be in the movie," says Dr. Danger.

"We're looking for monsters, aren't we?" I say. I look around the room. "Why did you run away from your undead daughter?" I ask the ghosts.

Silence on the recording.

"Have you seen Minerva Krackle?" I say.

"You think Krackle would be a ghost?" says Dr. Danger.

"If she is there, can she speak to us?" I say.

Silence in the room but again on the recording the word *No*. Then the words: *We didn't run away.*

"You are the mothers of Liz and Meggie, aren't you?" I say.

There's a moment of silence and then a rumbling, as if the whole house is building up its strength. We can hear this on the recording, of course, but we hear it in the room as well.

"I'll take that for a yes," I say. "But I'll ask again. Have you seen Minerva Krackle? Has she joined you on that side?"

Our Meggie is here. The voice on the recording sounds like multiple voices, but I don't hear any of the recording until later, until we are back in the car and driving away. *She was supposed to be here so long ago. We came here for her, so early, thinking she'd be here.*

Dr. Danger and I hold our breaths as the house rumbles again, as if letting out the energy of a great and powerful effort. I wait a few beats.

Minerva is not here, the voices say. *But pieces of her were left behind. Every interview she had. A small piece of her unlatched itself each time she absorbed someone else's story.*

"Do you know how she would end her movie?" I say.

She's everywhere if you look hard enough. But you have to look. You have to listen.

"Is there anything you regret from life?" I say.

"What kind of a question is that?" says Dr. Danger.

"A good one," I say.

The planchette on the Ouija board begins to move. On the recording the voices say *I wish I knew. I wish I'd stayed. I wish I'd run away a long time ago.* Dr. Danger and I let out little yelps of surprise despite ourselves as we hear the voices loud, right beside, almost inside our ears. The scraping of the planchette on the board as it moves to the letters D-E-A-T-H-I-S-A-C-O-N-S-T-R-U-C-T and then L-I-F-E-I-S-A-C-O-N-S-T-R-U-C-T and then H-A-H-A-H-A-H-A-H-A-H-A-H-A-H-A until I make it stop.

● ● ● ● ●

(2019) VIDEO

I fish the parts of my wings out of the trash – the pieces I had cut off for this film. I dig a hole on the hill behind Krackle's apartment building and bury myself in the dirt. I make a whole ritual of it. I say a few words for myself. I record the whole thing.

• • • • •

(2019) VIDEO

Dr. Danger agrees to this being the end of the movie, though he and I are arguing over the middle bits.

I keep the feather from my wing pinned to the wall above the editing bay. I give names to all the colors I see there.

I call Liz several times and leave messages, asking her to come to the film festival where the film is premiering. I record these calls and drop them, last minute, into the final moments of the movie, I guess, for some emotional tension, some hope or possibility. Documentaries don't always have an ending or resolution, exactly. Because there is, in the background, something still bubbling, a bigger question than one little story can answer. Are we going to show up for each other, or not?

I don't think Liz will come. She's long gone. After all, the film reveals to the world that The Great Merlan is still alive. And that monsters are real, to a degree. To the degree that they were always real, despite what we have always told ourselves. Despite the fact that we are, actually, very bad at recognizing when we meet, or become, the thing we fear so much.

That's where I landed with this film, anyway. Who knows how that first audience will take it all in.

Which is why I'm asking if Liz can be there—because I need an escape plan. The Great Merlan was an escape artist, when it comes down to it. And I'd feel better if she was there at this premiere. When I walk into the theatre.

We spend the last bit of Time we have before the deadline recording the growth of my wings, which also goes into the movie. I don't cut them back this time. And it hurts more than I could ever have imagined. They are bigger than they ever were, by the end. Even bigger than the version of them Liz let me see.

They keep growing even after we have to stop filming to wrap up the movie. And they keep growing in the weeks leading up to the premiere.

The part of growing after the deadline is not in the movie, but we record it anyway.

If not for a movie, at least for us. Because Time has a knack of slipping away from us, and we want to remember.

• • • • •

It's the day of the film premiere, and Dr. Danger and I have been hiding out in a small hotel room in the fancy mountain town, just down the street from the theatre. The film is screening right now, in fact. Dr. Danger is there to watch, texting me a countdown.

Dr. Danger is filming this bit. He leaves the theatre minutes before the end of the film, when he knows I'll be walking down the street. I have my jean jacket on, holes cut into the back to make room for myself. I don't try to cover them.

I emerge from the hotel and start walking.

There are men in monster suits and superhero outfits walking up and down the street, charging tourists a few bucks for a photo. They came to the festival knowing about the movie, about Krackle's big comeback. Looking to make a quick buck on all the monster bullshit.

Dr. Danger is outside the theatre, and I can see him, several blocks away, his top hat nearly falling off his head as he waves at me. I can see all of Dr. Danger's colors today. I just call them all Dangerous.

"Yes, I see you!" I say.

"This is highly melodramatic," says a voice to my right.

And I'd know that voice anywhere. Because it comes with the smell of chlorine.

"I'm pretty sure the Great Merlan did a similar thing in the eighties," the voice goes on.

I turn to see Liz beside me.

She shrugs. "That was before my time though."

I flick my wings, which have grown into the darkest version of themselves, but full of color, a sea of shades that multiply every time I look at them.

"So you want me to pull you out if things go sideways," says Liz, sticking her cigarette in her mouth.

"I thought it would be good practice," I say. "In case The Great Merlan ever makes a comeback."

"We both know she's dead," says Liz.

"Yeah, well, that's never stopped her before," I say. "Or Krackle for that matter."

"Can you fly with those?" she says, pointing at my wings.

"Maybe someday," I say.

Liz reaches out and touches one of the wings. I can feel Liz's fingers gliding over the feathers and the bone and the skin. My cheeks flush, and I see her face, too, go slightly pink. But a new shade of pink I've never seen before. One I name Liz.

I turn toward Dr. Danger and wave our signal.

He waves frantically back.

And so I make my way down the boulevard, letting my wings spread out as wide as they can go. I take my Time, walking among the costumed characters who have followed our rumor here, and the audience as they spill out of the theatre, their gaze turning toward me in recognition.

A few tourists who have no idea what is going on, who have not yet seen the movie, stop me and give me a few dollars for a picture, compliment my wings and ask where they were made. I ask them questions about themselves, but I mostly listen.

As I walk, I can feel Liz's Time wrap softly around me, at a respectable distance, just in case.

I manage to lift myself off the ground a few inches, before the raw skin on my back and the weakness of the wings get the best of me. It will take some Time to get used to.

ACKNOWLEDGMENTS

Thank you to Manuel Gonzales and my 2017 Tin House Cohort who saw and gave great feedback on the very first version of *Krackle* in the form of the longest short story I'd ever written.

Thank you to the Clarion Ghost class who have all made me a better writer and have helped me feel accepted in the speculative world. Especially to Sam who would never, ever call me quirky.

Thank you to Fernanda Vidaurrazaga, Alan Lin, Kate Weinberg, Ayize Jama Everett, Chloe Cole, Susan Straight, and Nalo Hopkinson who all saw some version of *Krackle* or stories connected to it and were foundational in getting this here.

To everyone at Split/Lip Press who believed in this little novella more than anyone, including me.

Two stories connected to the Krackle universe appear in *F(r)iction Magazine*'s ARCANA issue ("The Great Merlan Dies in Agony, Live On Stage!") and in *Bourbon Penn*, Issue 24 ("The Belly and the Trees"). Thank you to *F(r)iction* Editor-in-Chief Dani Hedlund for her thoughtful and detailed edits of "The Great Merlan..." which helped in no insignificant way in shaping what *Krackle's Last Movie* would become. And thank you to *Bourbon Penn*'s Editor-in-Chief Erik Secker for giving my weird stories a home since 2014.

Thank you to my parents, Jeannene and Steve, and my brother Zachary for always supporting me and my weird little stories. Mom, I promise I will write you a romcom some day.

And thank you to my partner John Paul who keeps life whimsical (there's a bird in the apartment).

CHELSEA SUTTON is a writer and theatre maker based in Los Angeles. She's a PEN America Emerging Voices Fellow and a graduate of the 2022 Clarion Science Fiction and Fantasy Workshop. Her short fiction has appeared in *Uncanny Magazine*, *Apex Magazine*, *CRAFT Literary*, *F(r)iction Magazine*, and *Bourbon Penn*, among others. She is the author of the flash fiction chapbook *Only Animals* (Wrong Publishing, 2024). This is her first novella.

CHELSEASUTTON.COM

NOW AVAILABLE FROM SPLIT/LIP PRESS

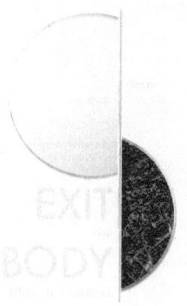

For more info about the press and titles,
visit us at www.splitlippress.com

Follow us on Instagram and Bluesky: @splitlippress

www.ingramcontent.com/pod-product-compliance
Lightning Source LLC
Chambersburg PA
CBHW020045030726
47499CB00007B/2588